CROSSING THE WATER

CROSSING THE WATER

The Alaska–Hawaii Trilogies

IRVING WARNER

Pleasure Boat Studio: A Literary Press
New York
2009

Crossing the Water: The Alaska–Hawaii Trilogies
By Irving Warner
ISBN 978-1-929355-51-8
Library of Congress Control Number: 2008941441

Design by Susan Ramundo
Cover by Laura Tolkow

Pleasure Boat Studio books are available through the following:
SPD (Small Press Distribution) Tel. 800-869-7553, Fax 510-524-0852
Partners/West Tel. 425-227-8486, Fax 425-204-2448
Baker & Taylor Tel. 800-775-1100, Fax 800-775-7480
Ingram Tel. 615-793-5000, Fax 615-287-5429
Amazon.com and **bn.com**

and through
PLEASURE BOAT STUDIO: A LITERARY PRESS
www.pleasureboatstudio.com
201 West 89th Street
New York, NY 10024

Contact **Jack Estes**
Fax: 888-810-5308
Email: *pleasboat@nyc.rr.com*

Contents

I. Alaska: The Lost River Trilogy 1
   The Gray Owl 5
   Robot Hunting 35
   Talk About Wolves 55

   The Bridge: Crossing the Water 81

II. Hawaii: The Island Trilogy 85
   Day Tour 89
   There Must Be Reptiles 123
   Old Okata 139

Part I
...
The Lost River Trilogy

Prologue

The river made no distinctions between good, bad, or indifferent. Each traveler had his own unique story, and what he was, had been, or was going to be had no mitigating effect on the journey before him.

1. The Gray Owl

i. The Road
Take a stick. Push the end of it into wet earth; draw a straight line, then stop; now turn a bit, keeping one line connected to another, draw another half as long. Look down at your work and you see the profile of a steeple, one side longer than the other, like this ___/ .

So this road went straight, took a jog north, proceeded another twenty miles and ended. Fifty-two miles total from the town to the end. This was the road Harriet Weir had traveled to the hairdresser every week for 28 years.

1.

The SUV broke down six miles from Lost River Hot Springs Resort. Actually, Harriet knew it was out of gas. Unsettled on departure, she'd forgotten to fill it. But now, even to the girl—maybe especially with her—she felt foolish admitting to this. She didn't like lies, but she lied anyway.

"We've been having mechanical problems with it."

Harriet got out, began to change into walking shoes while the girl looked nervously back toward the Hot Springs, then toward town—forty-seven miles distant. Harriet knew what was next.

"Where's the cell phone?"

"I left it at the resort."

"*What?!*"

She cast a hopeful look toward the Resort, then shook her head, confused.

"Well, it isn't that far back," the girl said. "I'd better stay with the car. I don't think I'm that popular back there."

She allowed herself a soft, nervous laugh. Harriet bent one leg up, removed a shoe, pausing on one leg before repeating the process with the other. She then shoved the cuffs inside her socks. Today, the bugs would be bad.

"I'm going on."

"Walking?!"

"Why, yes."

Harriet stuffed her in-town shoes in a small pack, then checked for bug dope. When she looked up and down the road, the only object disturbing its continuity was the girl—standing by the truck, looking first at her, then toward the Resort. Harriet began her walk at a fast pace. Behind her, she heard the girl running to catch up.

The gray owl first came to Harriet only during winter dreams. When she'd first moved to the Hot Springs after she and Otto were married, she'd told him about it, but he was never interested. Otto was a rationalist—didn't believe or analyze things unless they had substance. "Provability," he told her.

That was back when they'd discuss such things.

It was about fifteen miles to Pierce's, a deaf mute. Since he had no radio or cell phone, he wouldn't know. He did have two old pickups.

It was important for Harriet to move on, away from the Hot Springs. The girl was confused. Why would Harriet elect to hike on, rather than back—just a few miles? The first of the bugs quickly located the girl, and she talked while skipping along after Harriet, lifting one leg and slapping at bugs, then the other.

"But Otto, or even Weejee—could help. He'd help you, wouldn't he?"

"I shot Otto."

The girl stopped but Harriet walked on. In back of her, she heard the girl draw a breath. She still worked away at the bugs—the flats of her hands slapped bare abdominal flesh left exposed by her tank top and designer cutoffs. These were a perfectly inappropriate manner of dress on the road, back at the resort, or in fact anywhere in this part of the world.

ii. Topography
The form and shape of the land around the road was often described as rolling. To visualize this, imagine air passing under a light blanket, much like a bedspread at the moment it's tossed and settling over a bed. Or, even better, think of a sea with waves, great humps cruising along under a watery blanket, suddenly frozen, then transformed into earth—rock formations covered with coarse, sub-Arctic soils.

Such was the land surrounding the road, a panorama of monotonous, low, rolling hills. This had been Harriet's home since she and husband Otto settled there years before.

2.
While walking, Harriet struggled to put aside her problems and enjoy the straightness of the road—how it passed along through the stubby black spruce, then suddenly emerged upon an expanse surrounded by tall aspens and cottonwoods. These would lean wearily over the road. It was a Monday, and there were no cars out to spray gravel and rock as they sped by. She was grateful for that today. Harriet could walk along, concentrating on how cleanly the road passed through the land. As she walked down the road, her mind wandered—or meandered, like her father would say—and she was unable to overcome a confusion in time and place. Perhaps it was the fatigue.

The gray owl would visit only on nights when Harriet wanted Otto. This was in the early years, before the twins were born. It would appear, gliding through the narrow divide, then dip low, just above the small frozen watercourse between the hills—the beginnings of Lost River.

Harriet rested on the rail of the seventh bridge, which was really the second bridge, from the Hot Spring's standpoint. Everything worked by bridges out here, in regards to place and distance. Second bridge, fifth bridge. Bridges.

Cross the fourth bridge. New bridge. Old bridge.

Actually, that first winter—when they'd bought the Hot Springs—there were only two real bridges. The rest were makeshift. Tossed up, here, there, this way and that way by locals. No regulations then.

"You don't still have the gun, do you? I mean, you wouldn't shoot *me*?"

Harriet was unpleasantly surprised to see the girl. She had not walked back to the station, but instead caught up.

She flayed constantly at the mosquitoes and whitesocks, even reaching under her tank top, which was held well out from her flat abdomen by swelling, ample breasts.

She possessed Otto's favorite feminine form.

"Favorite Feminine Form."

Said with Otto's German accent, it always sounded funny. There had been so many "girls" in the past twenty-six years. Harriet struggled to remember this one's name. Dora? Yes, Dora.

"Don't be ridiculous, Dora. I hate guns."

"My name is Dara, not Dora."

"Dara, then."

Harriet drew a disappointed breath, pushed off the rail and walked away. She had enjoyed being alone on the road. Enjoyed its exquisite straightness.

iii. Road History

Central to life along the road and land was Lost River. In the early 1900s it earned its name when thousands of prospectors who'd come to the interior of Alaska lost bankrolls prospecting it. The Lost River yielded little gold from much labor resulting in thousands of worn backs and spent grubstakes. Later this era was romanticized in poem, ballad and story.

Nothing was written of the slag piles, giant mounds of tailings and tens-of-thousands of rusting, iron steam-points used to thaw through the permafrost. When Otto and Harriet came to Lost River Hot Springs, one of the old spas was overgrown with algae, and the other was empty and filled with garbage.

3.

It occurred to Harriet that during the last ten years, dreams were the only private world she had. At first she was ashamed of her dreams, which really only amounted to one or two variations of the same thing.

But that was wrong.

As she walked along, Dara trooping behind her, she reconsidered: Actually she did have one weekly time of privacy, didn't she? On her way to the hairdresser in Fairbanks. The night before, Otto had again worked it into his humorous nightly chat with the guests.

"Minus 40 and Monday, goes to ze' hairdresser. Snow like hell, she goes to ze' hairdresser. High season, resort full of wonderful guests, makes no difference, she goes to ze' hairdresser. At first, I think she has a lover in town," here he paused to let the guests laugh—most with growing embarrassment—then added, ". . . but no," and he gestured around—the resort, the European style dining room—nodded in admiration at what was mostly her doing. He shrugged and added, "*Gut am Geschaft, falsch am Geschlect.*"

In German, no less. And that had done it for Harriet.

Otto had sometimes kidded Harriet about her *sexlessness* in private—oh, maybe with a friend present, but never in the open dining room, before guests, and after the girl—Dora, or Dara—had made that ugly scene just an hour before.

The Professor had not laughed. Instead, he said something quietly to Otto in German—Harriet had not caught what it was. He then picked up and went to his suite, his wife Frieda—herself very famous—on his arm. Soon, the other guests—mostly his friends and relatives from Germany—followed. The fiasco, humiliation—and just plain shabby hospitality of it—were complete.

Horrible scene.

She had planned for the Professor's gathering since midwinter, going into every possible detail. Every *possible* detail.

"You know, you probably think you can walk me into the ground. But I ran the Boston Marathon, you know. Like, I've been working out since I was fifteen."

Harriet became angry thinking about the night before. Take the matter of wine: Very few German men knew French wine like the Professor, and Harriet had suffered bravely working with Goldstein and Farbers to surprise the Professor with a wine list he'd surely admire.

"You know, these fucking bugs are just about ready to devour me! I know you have bug repellent, so you're just enjoying every *minute* of this, aren't you."

Harriet struggled back from the wonderful memories, now so sullied, of last winter's planning. She stopped and turned. The girl looked at her angrily, reaching under her tank top, scraping away invading bugs.

"I didn't ask you to come along. And you know I don't allow my girls to go braless OR wear tank tops. Nor do I approve of obscene language. And I'm *not* enjoying anything connected with you. Here."

Harriet reached into her pack, took out the smaller of two bottles of bug dope, bent quickly at the waist, set it on the dirt road, turned and walked off. It took several minutes to return to her thoughts, but instead of the disastrous dinner, her mind diverted from it. It drifted elsewhere, to the old places. Respite. She needed respite from this day.

The river was frozen, only open at one of the numerous hotsprings along the steep, frozen banks. When the owl flew over this, the waters and land would thaw in its wake. As they thawed, a warmth spread over Harriet, light and sure, until it completely took hold, and she was visited by unparalleled energy, leaving her drawn and leaden.

Harriet watched the summer storm sweeping toward Lost River from the southwest. What had begun as clear, blue sky darkened as it moved toward the interior, having forced its way over the Alaska Range. This storm had energy, and soon lightning flashed and thunder was heard in the distance.

The wind moved ahead of the front, and at first the tops of the aspens, cottonwoods, and white spruce on the hill slopes began to sway. Ahead, as she crossed the sixth bridge, Harriet saw that for a summer storm, it had uncharacteristic depth to it, and that she'd need shelter, at least for the initial minutes. When the front would funnel down and steam roll across the lowlands drained by Lost River, there would be an initial deluge followed by smaller ones.

In her pack were a wind breaker and a rain bonnet. They would be enough for the light rain that would follow the first cloudbursts. When she left the road, threading her way along a lightly used path toward an old highway shack, she noticed a pair of woodpeckers dart past. They, like all other creatures, knew the storm was about to hit and sought cover to avoid a plumage-load of rainwater.

iv. Animal Life Along the Road

During the summer many types of birds bred in the countryside surrounding the road, even gulls, noisy visitors far from any sea. In the winter, bird life was limited to ravens, chickadees, a few grosbeaks, and small and large owls. There were a few others birds, but never as many as there were during summer months.

Moose, black bear, and snowshoe hare were seen often along the road. All were enjoyed by human inhabitants as table fare. More discreet were the predators. Wolves would rarely be seen by those on foot; from the air, they would scramble for cover single file, disappearing into thickets of aspen or willow.

Coyotes were seen somewhat more often, perhaps along the road attending to a recently killed snowshoe hare. Fox were seen less frequently than coyotes—shy creatures, themselves at risk of becoming a larger predator's meal. There was only one member of the cat family along the road: lynx. To see one of these richly furred hunters, even once a decade, was rare. Their large, cat tracks were always seen, though, usually in areas where hares thrived—when they thrived.

But the animals rarely seen—and never desired to be seen—were grizzly bears. Infrequent wanderers to the Lost River Basin, they were feared. The nomads—their vast keg-shaped heads frosted with white, their massive shoulders topped by a thick hump—got in cabins, absolutely ransacking them, and indulged themselves in no end of other nastiness. But they usually wandered off before being shot. Prior to that, their presence created controversy and spawned numerous leather-headed ideas for countermeasures. Grizzly, even when absent from the area, remained the Grendals of the road's beast legends.

At the very start—on her first week at the Hot Springs—Harriet began a list of animals she had seen, the dates they were spotted, and what they were doing. Even if she wasn't sure what it was—say, a small bird that came to her feeder—she noted it by description. These were her neighbors, her only neighbors, and she wasn't about to let them go unnoticed.

4.

Otto had joked about the girl's outrageous actions with the guests—this is how he'd begun his regular after-dinner routine of table-to-table social chat. He, of course, had not been in the dining room when Dara came in, and, while spewing obscenities at Penny, wrestled her to the floor just inside the kitchen. Everyone, of course, could hear—and knew.

After Otto's unexpected slight of Harriet, and the Professor's politic withdrawal to his room, she had gone to her desk in the kitchen, consulting her English/German dictionary to make sure she'd understood Otto properly. "Good at business, bad at sex." Yes, she'd understood, right enough.

The entire night horrified Harriet.

"The Professor won the Nobel Prize for Physics, Otto. It was his retirement celebration. The *indignity* of it all! Have we done all this work, for this!?"

"Joking is business. *Dieses ist Geschaft*, Harriet. Business! *Und* the professor? *Er ist ein miser.* That bitch wife of his will probably ask for a refund."

Otto sat on the end of the bed trimming his toenails, the final routine concluding his evening preening prior—she knew—to visiting the waitress who had prevailed in the struggle for his favors. Their bedroom smelled of bay rum, his favorite scent. Even under his turtleneck pullover, his muscles stood out, wonderfully defined. Except for slight grayness at the temples, which he dyed out, Otto looked not much older than when they'd come here twenty-eight years before.

If he would *only* have shown at least professional concern about it.

"Joking is not good business when it is at my expense. And he's not a miser. He's very generous. His generosity is our business, Otto."

On the way over to the house, she'd picked up the pistol Otto used to shoot squirrels who robbed their buildings of insulation. When she came around the end of the bed and aimed it at him, he put aside the nail clipper and looked sadly into the barrel. Putting a foot to carpet, he listened placidly while she said, "You've spoiled all my work for the last time," and she pressed the trigger. It did nothing. Otto pointed at the pistol, gesturing a semi-circle with his index finger.

"No. You pull the hammer back all the 'vay, *then* press the trigger. *Und*, it is unloaded, Harriet. As if you had stomach for such business."

He stood, finished dressing, inserted a red carnation in his lapel, and went out.

She sank to her dressing table chair, allowing the pistol to rest in her lap. Harriet remembered weeping for a bit, rare for her.

The gray owl's appearance became the harbinger of Pierce's arrival. The great bird would spread its wings, stopping just before the rim of the water tank above the hanger, and land so lightly it appeared to have just materialized there.

Pierce would ski down the road, his great upper legs sweeping along powerfully. As usual, the owl's arrival transformed the countryside to late spring, the time of leaf-out, and the arrival of warblers and swallows far from the south. Harriet would become confused: How could even Pierce ski so effortlessly across the snowless, late spring landscape?

The gray owl would turn atop the water tank, looking out at Pierce as he took off his skis. He kept his intense gaze on the house, almost at the very window where Harriet looked out. She would wonder, each time, why he was here.

And when she'd turn, perhaps to ask Otto—or tell Otto—that Pierce was here, Otto was gone. Lying on his side in their bed looking at her was Pierce.

She had cried herself out, then gone downstairs to the gun cabinet, sorting through various boxes of ammunition.

Finding the right type by trial and error—miniature-appearing missiles—she returned to the bedroom and sat back on the end of the bed and loaded the pistol. She waited there nine hours, until Otto came back to dress for the early morning horseback trip with the Stuttgart group.

"Did you kill him, Mrs. Weir?"

Since the old highway shack's roof was aluminum sheeting, Harriet could barely hear her over the tumult of the rain. Harriet sat on a milk box at the front door, looking out at the rain pouring through the tall grove of glistening white birch; each trunk reflected the indistinct glare of the sun that managed to filter through the steamy overcast. With the squall, the crowns waved sedately in ancient salute to passing weather. She struggled half-heartedly to take her attentions away from this scene.

"I don't see that as any business of yours, in view of the circumstances."

Harriet returned her attentions out the door and watched rain tumble down through the adjacent grove of white birch. The glint of diffused light, even through the overcast, caused this tumult of falling water to appear like a falls tumbling over a cliff—wished that behind it was concealed an entrance offering escape from this day's anguish.

Beyond this mystery of falling water, almost not visible in the rain storm, ran Ribbon Creek. It would join Lost River a quarter-mile downstream, losing itself in the wider, deeper river.

"Mother, just dump him. The place is worth millions. I know all sorts of lawyers..."

Harriet jumped. Tonya's voice seemed so immediate, she nearly answered; then she reminded herself, *I'm not myself. I haven't slept in two nights.*

Tonya, of course, hated her father, as did her twin Wila. The problem was, they—like everyone else—didn't know Otto, had not lived his exciting vision to establish a world class, two-star resort. He had been a young man, a survivor of the postwar rubble that had been Hamburg. Yet Otto realized almost three decades before it became a trend, that people—very wealthy people—would pay for experiences that produced more than ". . . hides on ze floor, skulls on ze vall."

"They said you and Otto had—had an understanding, about, you know."

Harriet turned wearily at the waist and saw Dara had removed her top and was lathering on bug dope. Turning back, she noticed the rain had turned to little more than a drizzle. She stood, picked up her pack—and after putting on her wind breaker and bonnet, ducked her head before walking from cover. Hesitating, she looked back and added, "Slathering it on just wastes it."

Harriet knew that going overland, along Ribbon Creek, then down a well-worn hiking path on the south bank of Lost River, would save two miles on the way to Pierce's. But she enjoyed far more walking along the road. Though narrow and dirt-surfaced, the road bed was a dozen feet above the surrounding flats, thickets, and tree groves. Walking along it reminded her of walking the railroad tracks out to the old quarry with her sister. That had been years and years ago, during vacations in Vermont. Good memories.

v. Enemies along the Road (#1)
The cold:
Its reign was between the equinoxes.

The cold moved into Lost River from the northwest, though it could utilize any direction when mood struck. Creatures variously flew south, dug down, made runways, harvested moss, ate gluttoously, made money, robbed insulation, chinked cabins and houses, put up any and all food, and, most of all, readied their young against it.

Fur, feathers, down, hides, nylon, rayon, dacron, wool, cotton, fiberglass, moss, even snow—and the very air itself—were marshaled against it.

The cold was always there, patient, waiting for any weakness, folly, or, best yet—a diminishing of spirit to continue.

The cold worked steadily through each hour.

Those who said there were no serpents in the far north had not been there . . . or were just wrong. The cold was a serpent.

5.

The force of the shot threw Otto against her French wardrobe, and, bouncing off, he fell to his knees, then to his side: "*Mein Gott! Sie haben mich beendet!*"

Frightened, Harriet jumped back as he wallowed for a second, then, amazingly, sprang up. He looked at her, eyes at that moment misting over. Since she'd shoved the muzzle into his chest, the front of his shirt had ignited, the material smoldered—burning from the muzzle blast. Blood seeped through at once. She still held the pistol.

"Killed? With my own pistol!? *Mit meiner . . . gewehr . . .*"

He collapsed, unconscious.

She dropped the pistol on the bed while walking out, went to the truck, and found the girl waiting. Weegee ran the weed eater close by, clearing an area he'd done the day before. He leered at the girl. None of the other waitresses—not wanting to face Harriet after the humiliation the night before—were around to see the girl off.

"I guess Burt is, like, working on the plane or something. I really have to meet the Seattle direct today. So . . ."

Even Weegee wandered away—to avoid possible questions. Yet Harriet knew their pilot Burt had gotten drunk.

He was carrying on in supposed secret with the pantrygirl and, in any case, wasn't fit to fly on this day, of all days. Rare behavior for him.

Harriet could have said much concerning the irony, stupidity, unabashed brazenness of asking her, of all people for a ride to town. She had said neither 'yes' nor 'no,' and just climbed in with her "town" things.

The girl had just tagged along, assuming a yes. As they drove through the mammoth entry gate, with its garish Bavarian design, it occurred to Harriet that Otto was either dead or dying on the floor of their bedroom.

The gray owl's outstretched wings transformed Harriet's world at Lost River Hot Springs from one of business and remote admiration to something immediate and joyful.

After a few years, the gray owl visited any time there was true night, which, during summer, was limited to a few hours. As always, the gray owl would alight on the old water tank across from the resort hall. It would stoop, straighten—then shrug its great shoulders, and for such a large owl, its hoot was quiet and tentative.

Looking back out, she'd see the gray owl drop off the tank, catch itself just above the surface, and with darting, quick wings fly off toward the wooden bridge, leaving her and Pierce together. He would take her shoulders, then carefully, almost shyly, turn her away from her vantage point at the window. Though his arms were as hard as the alder they fed into the chalet fireplace, his hands—or rather the palms—were supple and tactile. It not only made no difference that there was no connection between the Pierce of reality and the one who came with the owl, but this made the dream special and supremely private.

The second storm squall, not as voluminous as the last, had fortunately caught them as they crossed the fifth bridge. Years ago, it had been the first bridge constructed by the state. Under it was much room, though it smelt badly of urine where weekend fishermen relieved themselves.

"You know, I can't feature, like, living here year 'round."

Harriet shifted a bit on the rock. She resisted answering—what did Harriet care where this girl did, or did not, want to live year 'round?

The bridge shed rainwater left and right, creating tiny rivulets into the North Fork of the Lost River. The nesting swallows swooped aggressively around both women a bit, but soon accepted them, and darted in and out of the dozens of nests in the bridgeunderparts.

In earlier years, the Highway Department came by and hosed the nests clear. "Dirty," they told her when she went into town and complained. "You know, Mrs. Weir. Hard on steel. Accelerates electrolysis."

But they stopped. It always helped that Otto contributed liberally to each Governor's race. This time, it helped the bank swallows at the fifth bridge.

"I suppose you hate me. I guess I don't blame you."

"I don't hate anybody."

"Even Otto? You shot Otto."

"Not Otto. Not you. Not anybody."

This was intolerable. Rain or no, Harriet quickly put her bonnet back on, ducked down and climbed up to the road bed, continuing. It was just over two miles now to Pierce's.

Within a hundred paces, the rain slacked almost to nothing, and she loosened her windbreaker. Soon, the after-rain mugginess would bring out droves of mosquitoes and whitesocks. She would need another layer of bug dope but was hesitant to stop.

vi. Enemies Along the Road (#2)
Biting Insects:
Their uncountable numbers were the price exacted by the sun for its

brief appearance in late spring and summer. Jokes were made about them, yet they were not funny.

People applied diverse lotions, potions—wore nets, unseasonably heavy clothes in hot summer weather—even took injections—to avoid biting insects.

Jokes were still made about them.

In early hours, when most slept, planes flew about town and villages and sprayed. Following a brief time of unparalleled torment after intense hatches, even the most righteous and haughty activist said nothing, saw nothing. Instead, they enjoyed the death it brought to the tiny, unthinking bits of genetic misery.

The four-legged creatures along Lost River were driven mad. They would charge into the cold, shallow water, hiding their entire body, save nostrils.

Some kinds of biting insects laid eggs in animals' hides, which hatched into larvae that would digest their way inward, eventually weakening and killing the creature. Jokes were made about the biting insects, yet they were never funny.

6.
Tyrone drove by, heading uproad, just as they reached the sixth bridge. He was drunk. Next to him sat his old dog, snapping absently at bugs.

After a six-month struggle in the strange realm of sobriety, Tyrone had backslid. Harriet had heard as much. While he talked out the driver's window, he looked at the girl swat, writhe, and swear in an intensifying struggle with the bugs. An open bottle of liquor was wedged between his legs.

"Fuckin' bugs, eh? Needa ride, Harriet? I'm headed to town, too." Harriet gazed at Tyrone sadly, unable to respond. Tyrone just tipped an imaginary hat to them both and drove off at a snail's pace. The girl momentarily stopped her battle with insects.

"Like, *hello there*!? You're driving *away* from town, you know? God! Drunk and driving like that."

Like most residents along the road, Tyrone hated Otto but liked Harriet. There were reasons; everyone had reasons when it came to Otto.

Principally, Otto thought locals shiftless, and he used non-resident labor. But that wasn't all. Throughout the years Harriet looked on as he alienated first one local, then another. Otto became cast as The Heel opposite Harriet's Wronged Woman. Since morality plays were the stuff of gossip along the Lost River Road, Harriet and Otto became stars in the area's melodramas.

Once, on a flight back from their annual booking and promotional tour in Germany, Otto joked, "Vy don't ve switch roles, Harriet? You become the bad guy, and I the good. Like an opera, ya? Each vinter ve vill start putting on a different drama for the locals. An opera."

Pierce was the only local who came around still—who occasionally did odd jobs for Otto. Like Otto, he never drank to excess; like Otto, he was in perfect physical condition; but unlike Otto, Pierce was admired by the locals. Though always deaf, he had not always been mute. A year before Harriet and Otto's arrival, and according to local historians, during his first winter along Lost River, Pierce had attempted suicide, bungled it, and instead shot away his vocal cords.

The incident was now established Road Saga, and everyone could recite the legend of Pierce's stupefying thirty-mile walk down to Eighteen Mile holding a blood-soaked bath towel to the awful, gaping wound. He'd passed out fifty yards short of the first residence.

After that, he always wore a scarf or a turtle neck to cover the scar in public.

When they'd first come to the Hot Spring, she'd felt Pierce's eyes on her. But after the children, she'd immediately thickened. And since—she knew beauty had never been her trump suit—she never found him looking at her in that manner again.

This made developments even more curious—more inexplicable. When they talked during ordinary visits—him writing on his ubiquitous pad of paper, her speaking carefully, so he could read lips—it was always cordial. Neighborly. Pierce was always a good neighbor.

In the earliest hours of morning the gray owl called him away. Pierce was not deaf in the dream and immediately heard the owl calling from atop the water tank.

Pierce would take her for a last time, and, though hurried—it might be months before he'd visit again—the same incipient touch of energy would gather. It would spread outwards from her middle as if she'd spilt warm milk across her abdomen. Then this force would hesitate—as a great cat might, before it pounced—and in one power-filled motion, would strike, causing everything to curl and explode with instantaneous light.

She would lie there as Pierce covered her with the comforter and dressed. She felt a soft touch when he left—feather light, more a draft than a touch.

One morning, Otto looked at her during breakfast and said, "If you didn't eat before bedtime, you wouldn't have nightmares." Then he'd elaborated about methods to control her weight. By this time, they'd slept separately for years.

Harriet and the girl walked along a path leading through a low-lying area south of Ribbon Creek just where they would join the ATV trail into Pierce's. They had left the road a quarter-mile back. It was profuse with stubby trees and wetland vegetation, a place notorious as a hatching ground for bugs. Probably some of the worst along the Lost River drainage.

Harriet wished she'd brought a head net and trudged

onward, cupping her hand over her mouth to prevent from gagging on bugs. It was a struggle to breathe in the churning, vaporous clouds of them.

Dara gave up her struggle just a few minutes from the ATV trail and became hysterical: She spun, dervish-style, tearing at her hair where the myriad of biting flies and mosquitoes had become entangled.

At first she shrieked, followed by obscenities, but soon her vocalizations became labored croaks as she gagged on more and more bugs. With the continuing spinning and flaying at herself, she finally fell, rolled over and began alternately weeping and babbling. Harriet felt a wave of satisfaction, a surprising mean spiritedness she never admired in others, certainly never practiced.

This feeling vanished at once.

Harriet reached quickly into her pack, pulled out the windbreaker, still damp from the recent squall. She removed her bonnet, whose wide brim helped keep away the nastier biting gnats. While the girl struggled into the proffered windbreaker, Harriet applied some additional bug dope, handing Dara the bottle. The girl foolishly had squandered hers.

Both women worked quickly, silently. Though Dara zippered the windbreaker up to her neck, she did so with sluggish dream-slow movements. So Harriet stooped, and worked on the girl's bare legs, applying a thin layer of the chemical. When she handed the bottle up to her, Dara became more aware and went about completing her neck, face and hands. Still, her mouth hung open somewhat, and she looked off into the marshland, eyes fixed and vaguely resentful.

"This whole summer is such a fucking disaster."

When Harriet stood, the girl leaned forward, her forehead coming to rest on Harriet's shoulder. She wept. Harriet raised her arms to push her gently away, but instead held her arms in mid-air, then dropped them to her sides. Despite the bug dope, sweat, and tangles of bugs, Harriet could still smell a trace of that morning's shower rinse in the girl's hair, now incongruously covered by Harriet's rain bonnet.

It was all such a typical Hot Spring Tableaux: *Foolish Girl* is plied for sex by the *Charming, Villainous Boss*. Unwilling to share him with O*ther Girls*, she is soon sacked and sent home. The girl Dara now performed her way through a mystery play more foreign than if she were suddenly transplanted back through five centuries.

While patting her on the back, Harriet looked around, taking note of the trail. They were less than a half mile from Pierce's.

vii. Enemies Along the Road (#3)

Desolation:

It was the most successful hunter along Lost River Road. It did not depend on seasons, temperatures, hatches—anything. It might kill, but it often maimed. Desolation had the entire continuum to itself.

A list of its victims would be long and stretch back to prehistoric times, before there was a road, before there were mines, before there were clocks and calendars.

But with the road—then clocks and calendars figured in—Desolation began to make heavy inroads with people in the Lost River area. Yet, there came a day Desolation turned to Solitude. And then the former would move on sullenly.

Desolation couldn't efficiently stalk a potential victim if its presence was known. But it would be back, just passing through, to see, listen, and, more than anything, to feel, expert at probing out weakness, even the potential for it.

7.
They were expecting her.

Pierce came out from his massive cabin, built piecemeal over a period of years from stately white spruce. Behind him was a State Trooper, and Harriet realized the obvious—a helicopter had been called out to the resort by one of the employees—probably Laura, the hostess, who functioned as manager when she and Otto were gone.

Pierce had a concerned, even pained, look on his face. Harriet saw that the trooper didn't look like a peace officer who was about to make an arrest. As was recently his practice, Pierce used the blank sides of catalogue cards scavenged from the library to communicate and shoved the first one quickly for her to read. As always, Pierce never addressed her by name.

"I'm sorry, Mrs. Weir. Otto had an accident, but he's all right. They've taken him to town."

Harriet sat down on a defunct snowmobile, dizzy. The trooper came around Pierce, standing alongside him. He explained further.

"Lucky it was birdshot. Made a deep wound, but he was able to walk to the chopper, Mrs. Weir. He lost blood, but he's a tough cookie." When she looked up, the trooper anticipated her question. "He'd been shooting at parka squirrels. When he came up to dress, he put the pistol down, then covered it with his jacket. When he pulled the jacket off the bed, the gun went off. Single actions, left cocked. . . ." He shook his head ruefully.

"Went off?"

Dara's voice was a monotone. Harriet had forgotten about Dara. She stood by, looking first at the trooper, then Pierce. When Pierce fetched Harriet something to drink, all three respectively withdrew, perhaps to give her a few moments to gather her thoughts together. It was hardly necessary.

Actually, she didn't care if the girl told the officer the truth or not. Clearly, Otto had designed—as he had everything else at the resort—a story to cover the embarrassment, and that would be that. A disgruntled employee's word?

Certainly Pierce would know the story was manufactured. Otto's precautions with firearms were widely known. Though no hunter, he had great knowledge of weapons and took no chances.

Pierce handed her a cold soda, and Harriet drank deeply, concentrating on the ground where a large beetle detoured around her foot. This obstacle behind, it doggedly burrowed under a piece of loose kindling and was gone. She felt the cold liquid move downward, a welcome balm from the situation at hand. Now must she play the role of the fretful, worried wife? Thankfully, they again left her alone.

Even if she insisted the story was false, Otto would maintain his rendition of things. Harriet looked up hopefully, eager for anything to take her mind from what she must do, despite swearing never to consider divorce.

The surroundings were greatly changed.

It had been several years since she'd been to Pierce's, and she again marveled at what she and her daughters termed the "Gizmoship" of Pierce: Water systems, windmills, electric appliances—everything had been cobbled together from here, there, and anyplace.

All of it was engineered to the finest touch and most tedious detail. Neither had the era of the personal computer taken Pierce unawares. Even from her vantage point she could see him through his wide screen door, proudly showing the girl and trooper his newest computers, most scavenged in part or whole from nearby military bases.

When they left the house, Harriet noticed Pierce look on with interest when the girl lifted the back of her tank top to scratch bug bites—holding it up for somewhat more time than necessary. Pierce followed alongside her, and she smiled at him while reading one of his index cards.

For many years, Pierce never allowed her to remove the scarf which he wore—summer or winter—to cover up the terrible wound on his throat. But one night she was undressing him—they would be kneeling on the bed, each facing the other—when she went to remove the scarf, his thick arms raised, once again to stop her. But then, he stopped. It was indeed an ugly scar—thick, braided like a snake around his neck. She ran her fingers over it, and after that, this—removing of the scarf—became part of it all. When her fingers ran slowly over the scar, they would lean against each other, him taking Harriet completely around the waist, and drawing her against him.

Finishing her drink, Harriet set the empty down and saw that both of Pierce's pickups looked to be up and running. When the three approached, she asked, "Can I borrow one of your trucks, Pierce? I should get into town."

The trooper interceded.

"The chopper will be here shortly, Mrs. Weir. Wouldn't you want to come in with us?" He looked questioningly at the girl, then added, ". . . or, me?"

Pierce was about to start writing on a card, but the girl quickly explained: "Pierce asked me to stay over the night, then he'll run me in tomorrow morning. The New York Direct leaves then, and I won't have to connect through Seattle." She shrugged. "You know, that's a drag, and I want to, like, get myself together after today."

The trooper gestured toward town.

"Your daughter is waiting in town. Actually, she's pretty worried."

"Well, I'll be there in less than an hour."

There was the briefest of glances between Pierce and the Trooper, then Harriet was obliged to watch indulgently as Pierce gestured out operating instructions. At one time it had been a resort truck.

The girl handed her the jacket and bonnet. While Harriet opened her pack and put them in, she feared Dara expected her to show gratitude for not saying anything. Harriet stepped into the truck, and when she started it, remembered how cold a starter it was: It coughed and labored, and she would be forced to sit there for a minute or so, despite her eagerness to be gone. The girl stood close, and now the sound of the engine would afford cover to anything inane she might choose to say.

The girl stepped back when Harriet closed the door, but then came forward and leaned almost through the window.

"You are a really nice woman. I wouldn't have said anything, even if you'd killed him, Mrs. Weir. He's a bastard and doesn't deserve you."

The truck had nearly died halfway through her statement—something Harriet had feared. But, as the truck's engine ran better, the girl lifted her hand in a discreet wave and backed away.

When Harriet drove off, the truck nearly stalled, but moved on slowly until it responded fully and chugged its way down the ATV trail toward the road. In the mirror, she saw all three looking after her, standing in line, Pierce in the middle. She felt the indignity fall behind her with measureless relief. *Why,* she thought, *did everything have to become a melodrama in her life?*

What the girl had said, of course, was inappropriate, and as Harriet had told her earlier, no concern of hers in any event.

Otto was alive and she would not go back. If Otto had been dead, she would not have gone back either. Both the same.

viii. Aging along the Road
Along the road, toll gates existed which no one saw. Each time through them, there was a cost in time. It could be in days, months, weeks, years. But there was always a toll.

It was unfair that there was more than one toll gate, but living things never aged at the same rate. Each set of seasons, the living things that moved up and down the road did so with less agility and sense of limitless future. The road itself was not the timekeeper, but instead aged its inhabitants according to a relentless beat set in motion at the planet's birth.

8.
Harriet was planning what she should, and should not, tell her daughter when she was confronted by the sight of the elderly man and his vehicle parked in the middle of the first bridge.

She became disconcerted when realizing she'd been so lost in planning, she had no recollection of driving the distance between Pierce's and the first bridge.

The old man had parked in the middle of the bridge—by far the most elaborate along the road. He shuffled over to his dilapidated truck to move. While waiting at the approach to the bridge, Harriet suddenly felt the ponderous fatigue of sleeplessness sweep across her. While the old man tried several times to start his truck, she put her forehead to the steering wheel and felt events take her by the shoulders and press sleep down upon her.

Seeing the customary five-gallon jug of water in back, she removed a kerchief from her pack, got out, soaked it good, and stood there, dabbing it on her face. She heard the old man's truck start, then watched as he drove by and parked on the road behind her.

Dabbing her face with the kerchief again, she felt the air rapidly evaporate the moisture from her face and the coolness was sweet and immediate. The old man got out of his truck, and when his door stuck while closing, he gave it a kick. On the door was written *River Rat Cruises*. He was a peculiar figure, with bushy eyebrows and a dark angry countenance, and he wore baggy bib-overalls. He gestured toward the river and talked loudly while walking back out on the bridge.

"No water down in that river. It's the dams. Screw up a river."

She dabbed at her face again, and when she took the kerchief away once more, he was back—nodding at her.

"You're beat. Sleepy. Don't fight sleep. Let it come over you, lady. Just let it come. Sleep heals. Sleep heals all the daytime wounds."

He shuffled over to his truck, re-secured the lashing that held an extensively patched and re-patched canoe on a rack. Harriet, who ordinarily would be put off by such familiar address, was not. Once again enjoying the coolness, she watched as he finished, then tendered a final dismissive gesture toward the river.

"I've canoed them all. Rivers, you know. Big. Medium. Small. This one?! It's a piker. Not my type of river."

Then he got in his truck and motored off. Clearly, he was a foolish person; there were, of course, no dams on Lost River, and anyone familiar with rivers knew they were usually low during the late summer.

Despite all, Harriet found herself smiling briefly. She walked onto the bridge and looked down into the river.

The riverbed was strewn with giant and medium-sized boulders, each one crusted with algae and such, dried after the receding waterline had exposed it to the long summer sun.

This bridge was the largest along the road, and at midpoint a good fifty feet above the river. Harriet walked along the downstream rail, and looked down river at the familiar sandbar where, years ago, she would take the twins to dig in the sand—a poor substitute for when she was a girl and her parents had taken her to Cape May.

She and the twins would park below the bridge, then thread their way down a narrow trail to it. The best days, as always, were those with a stiff breeze coming down the river from the headlands. This would limit the bugs and give the twins peace from not only their annoyance, but the layers of chemicals spread over themselves as a defense.

On the north end of the sandbar were two tall snags, old cottonwoods now crownless—hulking giants, clawing at the sky. She and the twins would watch woodpeckers and brown creepers dig out grubs, and their afternoon away from the resort would pass gently and memories of them remained special.

Looking that way, her eyes immediately fastened on the figure of a large bird atop one of the snags. She knew at once it was a Great Gray Owl, only her second sighting of one. Harriet was just correcting herself—about real sightings versus others—when the owl leaned forward, launched in her direction and descended rapidly to the sand bar, talons extended. Hovering momentarily, it latched its talons onto a rabbit, already dead, and attempted flight. But the burden was too large, and the huge owl was only able to carry it a few feet, before dropping it. Since rabbits would not be on the sandbar, Harried assumed the owl had dropped it there earlier as well, probably en route to its nest.

It flapped deeply, circling once again; its great strength allowed it to climb quickly, until it was level with Harriet on the bridge. Then, wheeling on a wingtip, it returned to the snag, alighted carefully on the smallest of branches, and shrugged its wide, slate-colored shoulders.

It looked down intently at its dropped prey. This potential feast now was a problem. Harriet saw the owl had not come close to getting the animal aloft. Frustrated, it shifted about restlessly on the branch.

And at that moment Harriet nearly fell backwards when, emerging below her a few feet from under the bridge, another gray owl loomed into view.

This bird was the larger of the pair, and before Harriet could draw another breath, it flew low over the sandbar, attached to the hare, and with deep powerful strokes of *its* wings indeed became airborne. Then, in a deft mid-air move, the bird adjusted its hold on the rabbit. Now, instead of the hapless animal facing broadside to the direction of flight, the move shifted it end first, offering less resistance. In a moment the owl climbed even higher.

Though unable to rise to the level where its mate sat, it was able to gain several dozen feet, and, maintaining this height, spirited its burden away downriver. Taking wing, its mate wheeled, and flew behind, and somewhat above its mate. Within a few seconds the owls rounded a bend and were out of sight.

At that moment, Harriet dropped the soaked kerchief. She watched as it fell; spinning downward, the checkered pattern of the cloth became a blur. Halfway down, it opened, and fluttered along. Finally, it came to rest on the largest of the boulders. It seemed beautiful when it fell, silent and coming to rest so gracefully. To rest.

Harriet renewed her grip on the bridge rail and looked back to the truck. Rest. To rest. It had been, she thought, almost two days since she rested.

Harriet looked in the direction where the owls had gone while walking back to the truck and getting in. She reached to start the truck, then hearing the engine, realized it had been going the entire time.

She drove slowly onto the bridge, paused, and looked one more time downriver, then drove off the bridge.

In a few miles, she'd see the first human habitation along the road. Then, a mile after that, the dirt and gravel surface would give way to asphalt, and it would be like driving anywhere.

The last dozen miles into town were the easiest and most uneventful. Her daughter would want to know everything but would—must—wait. At this moment, nothing seemed more vital to Harriet than the deepest and quietest of sleep. The old man might not know rivers, but he did know sleep.

2. Robot Hunting

i.

She struggled down Lost River Road. Her great hips swung awkwardly beneath her robe, its floral pattern soiled with hunks of mud, toilet paper, and feces.

Despite its being mid-spring, the dirt surface of Lost River Road was still frozen from cold nighttime temperatures, and her bare feet, uncharacteristically small and delicate, were cut and bloodied.

Earl Deets looked up from unlocking the Self-Serve pumps, and saw her go down hard, sprawling headlong onto the stiff, frost-bound mud. Her robe flew open, and when she rolled half over, Earl saw she was naked.

He shouted for Margie, then at the same moment ran downroad, taking his coat off while in motion. When Earl reached her, he saw that it was Mrs. Munson. Her hand reached straight up as if she intended to claw the skies themselves, and seeing Earl, she cried out, "Save yourselves! Edgar's gone crazy and tried to kill me." Her hand then clutched Earl so powerfully she nearly tore his shirt away. "And... and Mother of God, he's got my Charlie!"

• • •

ii.

Edgar gave up looking for Charlie. Being just seven, and slow-witted anyway, the boy would not understand.

Edgar returned to the cabin and had just completed loading all his firearms and ammunition into the camper when he realized his folly. Their armor, made from an amalgam of uranium and copper, would render all his weapons useless, save for the largest two. After putting the rest back inside, Edgar started the truck so it would warm up and defrost. He then went back in, took a box of saltines and a tin of jam from the pantry, sat at the table and opened both.

Since the argument had begun before breakfast, Edgar hadn't eaten.

Hungry. He was proud to be hungry. Humans became hungry. That was a critical point.

Edgar ate his fill and was tapping the lid back on the can when Charlie shuffled into the cabin, still wearing his Star Wars pajamas.

"I'm hungry, Dad."

Edgar smiled and began to pry the tin back open.

"Of course you are, Son."

• • •

iii.

Tyrone was always sure that weeping in front of Betts had cost him his marriage. While he shuffled alongside the swollen Lost River toward his tiny mobile home, he tried to remember when and where that had been—when he'd wept.

Bozeman, Montana? Wasn't it about halfway through his stint with the U.S. Marshal Service? Tyrone steadied himself against a log, then decided to sit for a few minutes. He stared hard into the yellowed flood water of Lost River, reflecting. He struggled to remember his way through three weeks of hard drinking, deciding it was probably Montana, all right.

But that didn't tell him the When. That remained hazy, but remembering the Where was Bozeman indicated it was far more than halfway through his thirty years as a Deputy U.S. Marshal. For Betts was his third and last wife, whom he'd met after Jo; she'd moved with him to Bozeman from Seattle, which had been a disaster.

He struggled with a swirl of names—for places and women: *Jo* had been the disaster, not Betts whom he'd met at an AA meeting. Jo was strictly a big city lady, while Betts was into canning, PTA meetings, and worrying about those two daughters of hers.

A panicky feeling came over Tyrone when it occurred to him it could have been Betts who'd found him curled up weeping. He thought it had been in their garage—the spot where'd he'd hide when things got gritty—the collision between memories and "barrel scrapings," which is what his father called the D.T.s.

Suddenly he was sick. The nausea had been hitting him in waves all morning.

Looking up after retching, Tyrone was surprised to see he still wore slippers. Amazing. He'd been blundering around in the woods since, well—he didn't know how long, but it was dark when the first of the black men began emerging from the woods around his trailer. Jesus, God, it had been dark, but he could see each one, the rope still around his neck—squeezing each, as rawhide might the neck of a leather poke.

Jesus, God and all the Saints put together, those hallucinations were the worst barrel scrapings.

Tyrone shuddered with the late spring chill. He was soaked, cold and absolutely dehydrated, which was causing all the problems.

Sweat.

He was drenched in river and creek water from thrashing around in the woods, then his own sweat—booze sweat.

"When you detox, Tyrone, for God's sake drink liquid. Lots of it, or you'll die."

Orange juice would do the trick, and if he didn't have any in the trailer, he'd try and get the Buick started and drive down to Deets'. First, he had to rise. He did so by punching first one arm into the ground, turning around and facing the log, then putting the other against it and pushing up jackknife style.

Yes. Liquid. If there was one doctor who knew his beans and bacon about coming off a hard, three-week binge, it was

Doc Floyd. The physician had lost ten times more than most because of the booze, and when Doc Floyd said it, there was more authority behind his words than with ordinary doctors.

Another wave of nausea and vertigo struck, but this time Tyrone managed to stay upright. He leaned into a spruce trunk, clinging hard. "Jesus God, man. What in hell are you doing living out there?"

He tried to remember who'd asked that. Well, in fact most asked that—most who cared. His legs went rubbery, and for a second Tyrone thought he might skin down the raspy trunk to the ground, but he held. Even at sixty-two years of age, Tyrone still had remnants of the old, grim strength.

When he was working the Styxsville lynchings, he'd been 6' 3" and had weighed two hundred and fifteen pounds, solid.

"You're tall enough to cut them nee'gras down without a ladder, boy."

The Mayor of Styxsville, his breath so reeking with liquor and chaw it nearly gagged him, had chuckled this observation when Tyrone and Parnell were moving him. They, along with those two useless FBI agents, scared to the core, cuffed the Mayor and hustled him across the Mississippi state line into Tennessee. There, even Federal lawmen felt healthier.

For the first time in hours, he noticed Queenie following behind him, struggling to keep up. She'd been doing that for sixteen years.

She too was wet and muddy and occasionally would shake with the chill. Suddenly the old guilt of the booze caught hold, and Tyrone felt terrible about the dog. Once again, she had stuck with him, no matter what was going on. He was about to reach down and pet her but caught himself—he was too unsteady for that.

Best stay upright, then get back, dry Queenie off—start the Buick if possible, and fetch some groceries down at Deets'. He looked upriver, then downriver, and Tyrone felt grateful for the return of his directional sense, for when the D.T.s hit and he fled like he had this morning, all sense of direction flew up the stack.

• • •

iv.
When Edgar drove up to Mr. Pierce's cabin, Charlie had fallen asleep under his down vest. When he got out of the truck, he looked in at his son, realizing how miserable a world it was—one that would be unbearable for poor Charlie, slow-witted and unused to any sort of meanness. It would be a poor parent who would subject his child to such unhappiness.

Edgar grabbed the shotgun and shifted the vest so it would cover Charlie's legs, and he closed the truck door softly so as not to wake him. He then went looking for Mr. Pierce—or rather, the robot that inhabited Mr. Pierce.

"Mr. Pierce! It's Edgar Munson. Your neighbor."

Edgar realized that he'd loud-hailed a deaf mute and smiled at the irony of it. He clanked a shell into the chamber and walked up the stairs of Mr. Pierce's great, white-spruce cabin. There would be no sense in knocking.

Inside he kept the shotgun at ready, playing it over the tops of the computers, and other such equipment that had possessed Mr. Pierce. He walked through the large main room into the back bedroom, moving with all caution. Robots were notorious for their telemetry systems—motion detectors, heat sensors—there was little in the way of such abilities they lacked.

If Pierce had been home he would know what was happening and would be waiting in ambush for Edgar. He moved through the bedroom and noticed the backdoor was bolted from the inside. That was out. It was doubtful even a robot could bolt a door from the outside. Pierce couldn't have gone out there.

He spun around, sensing a presence. An infinitesimal

portion of his finger touched the metal of the trigger. Edgar could feel its grooved inside surface and with pleasure inhaled the sweet acrid aroma of gun oil.

Raising the weapon, he sighted down the barrel and moved suddenly back into the front room, swinging the gun swiftly left, right, and straight ahead. But everything was quiet.

Edgar had guided dude hunters for over twenty years and had been in countless second-by-second situations where success, injury, or even death were measured in milliseconds, so he was pleased to note that his heart wasn't even beating hard. It took professionalism to survive in that setting. And now, today, it would serve him well.

He went over to the front door and ducking down, looked out the front window. Everything was quiet.

Backing over to the wood stove, Edgar didn't need to check; he could see and feel it was cold. Out. But how long?

Quietly, he opened the stove, yet kept a wary eye on the front porch. Moving his hand inside, he touched the coals cautiously. They were cold; there had been no fire since the day before.

Pierce was gone, probably in Fairbanks. The nights were still well under thirty degrees and required a fire. Edgar ejected the shell from the chamber, and palmed it back into the magazine. Walking back out, he inspected the hasp on the front door, smiling as he looked at the open padlock hanging uselessly. That was just like Pierce; of course robots would hardly care about security.

Edgar sat on the top step and put the shotgun aside. It was hard being alone, even though he did his best thinking alone. It was at the start of last winter when Estelle had gone into town for a week. Then he had time to reason his situation through. He became convinced that the world banking community had perfected their plan to replace all human beings with robots. The plan had been revealed to him in Munson's numerous credit card statements. Each, unlike before, had strange codes on them, and once decrypted—which took him most of November and December—had revealed the truth.

"Dad. I'm still hungry."

Charlie stood at the base of the stairs. Hugging the vest around him, he looked vacantly past his father. "Is Mr. Pierce here?"

"No, son, he's gone."

Edgar picked up his shotgun, took Charlie by the hand, and returned to the truck.

"I'll start the engine. Best to keep warm, son. You only got over the flu last week, you know. Mr. Tyrone will know where Pierce went."

He backed off a ways, turned, and drove down the old ATV trail toward the Lost River Road.

"Dad, is Mom a robot?"

"Of course not, son."

"Then why did she hide down in the outhouse hole?"

"Well, your Mom and Dad had an argument, and with married people, that happens. It just happens." Edgar smiled remembering that morning, "I should have looked there first, if I would have thought."

Charlie settled into the candy bar that Edgar gave him, and Edgar smiled as the boy unwrapped it. Edgar had one more candy bar and some salmon jerky, and that's all Charlie would want, really. He was a quiet, undemanding child, and, save for his slowness, had been a joy.

• • •

v.

Actually, Tyrone's trailer had been downriver, not upriver, and because of delays atop delays, Queenie gave up on ever finding home. It took a half hour and enduring several waves of sickness for Tyrone to coax the old dog up. He was too damn weak to carry her, as he had so many times. So, when they did emerge from the woods into the small clearing where his dingy blue trailer sat, he was unpleasantly surprised. He recognized Munson's old camper at once, and the last thing he expected or wanted were guests. Especially Edgar Munson.

Shuffling around stumps and brush piles, he reconsidered; it could be the makings of a lucky break, because he could give Munson some gas money for running down to Deets' to fetch supplies. Starting his Buick was going to be tough, even if he did manage it. Yes, it was a lucky break.

Placing both hands on the handrail, he took a rest before taking on the four steps up to his small landing. Jesus, Tyrone could use a lay-down, and he had to get liquid in him. But that would be another benefit, wouldn't it? He could catch a lay-down while Munson went to and from Deets' store.

Like most along Lost River, Tyrone had an open-door policy, and rubbing his hand hard across his face, considered that he would not want to walk in unexpected on the eccentric Munson. When he managed a "Hello!" his voice croaked miserably, and what came out sounded sheep-like.

He took each step one at a time, remembered Queenie, and looking behind saw her standing—front paws on the first step, back paws on the ground—considering yet another obstacle for the morning. But, giving a protesting groan, she followed—and soon was on the landing next to Tyrone. Opening the door, Tyrone walked in, smelling the stink of his neglected garbage, feeling at once ashamed and irritated at having to apologize for something else. He was always apologizing.

In the thirty-six-foot-long trailer, Tyrone knew at a glance that Edgar wasn't inside. Ordinarily, he would duck outside and call out to the camper. For whatever reason, Munson could be asleep inside; otherwise, he might have hiked off somewhere, anywhere. But Tyrone was too weak to worry about Munson and hoped that somewhere in the tiny kitchen he'd overlooked something to drink. Lurching forward, he stumbled against his half-dozen empty water jugs, nearly falling; the empty containers rattled loudly off the baseboards .

Jesus, why couldn't he have running water like most of America?

Tyrone was about to start looking in the cabinets when another wave of nausea struck—weaker than earlier ones, yet hard enough. Putting out his hands, he braced himself against the sink and waited it out.

• • •

vi.

Edgar sat on the banks of Lost River and watched Charlie arrange a half-dozen old sticks into military formations atop a log. Edgar smiled, but the smile vanished at once.

He traced the checkering on the shotgun stock with his finger and continued to think about the misery and sadness that filled the world, not the least of which was the plight of poor Tyrone. Edgar had followed the old dipso's tracks all about the woods and saw early on he'd been drunk to distraction, and sick—and most likely "in the grip of the snakes," as his own father had so often.

Yes. The bottle held Tyrone in its grip as it had his father. Remembering his father gave Edgar reason to sit awhile; plus, it would let Charlie rest, for the boy was no woodsman.

"Dad, is Mr. Tyrone a robot?"

Edgar looked over at Charlie, noted his cuffs had come out from inside his mudder boots. Putting the shotgun to one side, he went over and, brushing off mud, talked into the boy's left ear while stuffing each cuff back in.

"Robots aren't boozers, Charlie. So, no. He's not. Now keep those cuffs in, son."

He returned to the gun, sat and looked at Charlie as he played with his stick-toys. Edgar knew men had to make and follow through with tough decisions, and only slackers did not. What sort of a world could Charlie look forward to where the rich and strong always had their way? Even if Charlie had been normally endowed, mentally, it would be difficult.

Estelle talked nonsense when it came to special schools and such. Charlie would be picked off like a mouse in the midst of a bare field. What the rich and powerful could not do themselves, they shunted off to the robots.

"Dad, what sort of fish live in this river?"

Charlie was always fascinated by the river and was forever asking Edgar about the fish in it. The boy looked toward the river, its swollen spring waters dark with tannic acid, debris and even chunks of ice from upriver. It was an ugly river now, Edgar decided.

"Oh, all sorts, son. Suckers. Suckers live in that river."

Charlie nodded, concentrating on the dark, swirling water—as if he might conjure up a few by just hoping. Edgar stood and looked at his son, knowing that for weeks now, he'd mined all avenues of choice to the very bottom. Fact was, Estelle could never make a hard, loving choice about anything, especially Charlie.

He lifted the shotgun up from the log, and in an abrupt snippet of memory the image of a newborn Charlie being cradled against Estelle's great, sweaty bosoms came to mind. That was seven years ago, well before she'd become a robot. Edgar suppressed a moan, for this was an awful truth. Edgar could never muster enough heart to tell Charlie the truth about Estelle.

All in a second, the same sharp, acrid smell came to him in the soft downriver wind that also came to Charlie. The boy looked up at him.

"What's that smell, Dad?"

Edgar tested the wind several times, nodding.

"Starting fluid, son. Somebody's trying to start a car. Probably Tyrone."

• • •

vii.
Tyrone couldn't start the Buick, and threw the aerosol can of starting fluid aside in despair.

Despair.

He leaned against the car, feeling the old helplessness—of falling without hope of ever landing—returning in place of the nausea. Like most people, he was not in control of much, but he—even less than others. Tyrone had recovered from way too many binges in his life, especially since retiring from the U.S. Marshal Service. He could have worked on, but the boss had asked him to go.

"You're a good Marshall, Tyrone. But you must crawl out of that goddamned bottle."

All in the same moment Tyrone saw the envelope clipped against the windshield under the Buick's only wiper and Edgar Munson and his son emerge from around the end of his car. Without wasting a motion, Munson picked the envelope from the windshield and handed it to Tyrone.

"Note for you. Any luck with the car?"

Tyrone held the envelope, then used it to point downroad, toward Deets'.

"No. I'll give you some money for your trouble if you'd get some supplies for me down at Deets'. I'm under the weather, here."

Tyrone noticed the bush gun for the first time—a sawed-off shotgun for close work when an animal ran off wounded. He recalled Munson's being some sort of guide. Munson motioned to the envelope.

"It's marked *urgent*. That note."

Tyrone hadn't the slightest interest in this or any note.

Now that the nausea was passing away, a desperation for water or any liquid was taking hold so unyieldingly, it overpowered all.

"It can wait. I'm dry. Need fluids. If you want, I'll ride along. Like I said; I'm under the weather."

Tyrone minded his language, aware of the Munson boy. Actually, with the entire Munson household, that wasn't a bad idea, anyway.

Munson glanced at the boy, raised his free hand and ran it through the boy's hair; he then took him gently by the shoulder and turned him.

"Charlie, go to the car, son. Climb under my vest—catch some sleep. You were up all night."

The boy did as directed, and Munson smiled and shook his head.

"A good child, that boy," then he pointed toward the note. "That's an official envelope from the State Troopers, Tyrone. I hate lies, so I'll be straight with you. I'm afraid Estelle has run off to Deets' and called the law. Early this morning. So, I best not go down there. I'm looking for Mr. Pierce. Have you seen him? "

"What happened?"

"Well, like Pierce, she turned into a robot, and I'm giving you fair warning about that, because I know you haven't. You know, turned into a robot." Munson looked back in the direction of the camper. "But I tell you, I have a couple six packs of pop in the camper. Would that help slake that thirst?"

"It would."

"Well, it's under all my stuff. But why don't you go in, and I'll fetch it."

Tyrone managed his front steps again and wondered just what in hell he could do. Stepping around Queenie—now asleep in her basket—he sat on one of two stools at the trailer's only table. He hadn't seen or used his service weapon in over two years, and when he had, it had been during an attack of the D.T.s. Tyrone, horrified by the appearance of the lynched black men, shot up the entire clearing from inside and outside his trailer. Pierce, seeing what he'd done, took the gun.

Pierce: Now there was a damned good neighbor and human being who'd always helped and never looked down at people. Yes—always helped.

Tyrone labored to clear away mental cobwebs—processing the odd set of circumstances fate had dealt. Munson came in with the pop. Opening one for Tyrone who took it and for a moment forgot all else. Drinking the liquid, his throat worked in spasms. Once he downed some, Tyrone waited, hoping it would stay. Munson sat on the other stool and slid the shotgun on the table.

"My father used to get the snakes bad. Would go to the bathroom in his britches. Pretty disgusting." He looked sadly at the door, propped one elbow on the table, and rested his face in his hand. "Yeah, pretty sad, that. Now I'd never do something like that to Charlie. It is so tough to know you've brought even a normal child into this nest of vipers, and now these robots." When Munson looked back up, Tyrone saw he'd begun weeping. ". . . It would be too much for any boy. And Charlie, well, Tyrone, Charlie's kind of slow, anyway. He wouldn't stand a chance."

He put his head back in his hand and wept without embarrassment. It was a strange, quiet weeping. For several minutes nothing was said. Tyrone—ordinarily discomfited by anyone crying—watched helplessly, realizing the shotgun was only inches from his grasp. His best move—if he had still been capable—would be to grab it and crack it over the lunatic's head. But Munson was a big bruiser, and Tyrone was no longer even remotely possessed such strength.

He drank more from the pop.

"Actually, Munson, Pierce is down by the river. Do you want

me to take you there? I mean, if he's turned into a robot...."

Munson looked up, wiped his eyes and nodded.

"I'd appreciate it. I'll wake Charlie."

"Is that necessary?"

But Munson stood, picked up the gun and went outside. Tyrone hadn't thought he'd wake the boy and take him along. Any chance to decoy Munson, he supposed, had been better than none at all. Pierce, he guessed with relief, was still in town. But now what?

He looked down at Queenie sleeping; her old rib cage rose, then fell with the deep sleep of seventeen years. Tyrone's head was clearing fast, so he risked bending and ran his hand over the animal's flank. Even up to her twelfth or thirteenth birthday, there wasn't a squirrel that could call itself safe in Queenie's vicinity.

Tyrone stood and, out the window, saw Munson walking hand in hand with the boy back to the trailer.

•••

viii.

His genuine frailness gave Tyrone an excuse to stop frequently and think. Munson followed behind with the boy, and when they reached Lost River, Tyrone turned upriver. He didn't know why—either way seemed equally futile. He stopped frequently to catch his breath, sitting as long as he dared.

The boy would leave his father's side, go to the river, and look into the debris-filled runoff, asking what sort of fish lived there. Each time, Munson would answer the same. But he was becoming impatient with their objective.

"What's Pierce doing up here?"

"House logs. Before the pitch rises. Cuts and barks them way off where nobody can steal them."

Munson nodded, fielded another question from the boy

about trees while they continued. As Tyrone anticipated, they intersected an old road that at one time went back to one of many gravel quarries scooped out for construction of the road. These were now ponds and favored places for moose—and in the autumn, moose hunters. This particular road was also used in the summer by fishermen looking for holes off the beaten path. Also, since there was a very low bank on this side—in fact, something more like a beach—canoeists and kayakers with local knowledge favored it as a launching place.

Tyrone pled fatigue and sat before an improvised fireplace made from river rock—a miniature amphitheater. In the shade of it, ice still remained. Within minutes, they heard the approach of a vehicle—its shocks and springs squeaking terribly. Munson turned toward it, lifting the gun. This move allowed his coat to come half open, and Tyrone noticed the pistol and a bandoleer studded with brass cartridges.

Munson frowned, glanced to where his son stood at the river's edge, then at Tyrone. There was no time to do much else, and Tyrone watched with regret as a black truck with an old camper shell bobbed, jerked, and swayed its way around the bend, passed by the end of the quarry pond, ground laboriously over a last bump, and stopped. Generous wisps of steam from an overheated radiator hissed from the grill.

An elderly man opened the door upon which was written "River Rat Cruises." He hung his head out and announced, "It's running a little hot," then with a frown, glanced at the boy, then Tyrone, seated before the fireplace, and, finally, Munson. He was a curious figure with bushy eyebrows and a dark angry countenance. He'd been hanging about Lost River Road since the thaw. Several times, he'd had words with Deets about his prices, which Tyrone knew was common enough. Their new arrival reached into his bib overalls, fished out a plug of tobacco, and took a bite, tearing the piece away with ferocity. Despite this, he talked around it without audible impairment.

"What you hunting this time of year with that fool thing?"

Munson, whose frown had switched to a look of curiosity, took several steps toward the old man, then glanced toward the truck. Lashed to the top was an old canoe, extensively patched and re-patched. It was painted black, and it, too, had "River Rat Cruises" painted across the side of it.

The old man looked at the boy, then out at the river. At this location, it was wide—and discolored strangely with spring run-off. It swept by in sheen-covered bands—one dark, another darker yet, then a third of entirely lighter colored water. It was so far upriver, the river's forces had not thoroughly blended the runoff from diverse rivulets and melting swaths of winter snow on the ground and in trees.

He smiled, and hopped a bit with clear pleasure.

"My cup of tea. Now this is a river. This is water a guy can get his canoe into."

He turned and began to unlash the canoe. Munson looked carefully at the man, taking several more steps toward the truck. Charlie moved by him and didn't notice the concern on his father's face, nor his belated attempt to catch hold of him.

"Mister, you going to canoe in that river?"

"I am indeed."

He answered without looking back from his work, and Munson finally took Charlie by the shoulder and swept him gently until he was behind. Tyrone pushed up from his seat, and though initially his voice failed him, when it caught, it caused all three to look his way.

"Actually, Munson, this is lucky. Pierce is on the other side—you know, where that big grove of white spruce is, south," he pointed vaguely in that direction, "... over there."

The old man turned, frowning—and put a hand out to stop Munson from speaking.

"If you think I'm shuttling you across for nothing, you're

both just about as wrong as can be. I've canoed them all. Big. Medium. Small. This one!? Piece of cake for me, even though it's up and angry. Rivers don't scare me. Never have!"

Munson looked the strange old man up and down, and Tyrone's insides tightened: How would he explain Pierce being across the river? But fate and luck were dumb things, and Tyrone, if he had learned anything, had lived that. Munson gestured to the water with the shotgun.

"Mighty swollen. Swift. Sure you could manage us?"

"Well, I can. But how about you? You ain't getting in the middle, then going chicken on me, are you?"

The old man smiled smugly and began turning the canoe about, to remove it from the rack. Tyrone fumbled with his wallet, and brought out a twenty, handing it to the old man. He stared at the bill suspiciously, then glanced to Edgar who looked back with a mixture of stubbornness and confusion. He yanked a tie-down loose.

"Here, pilgrim, hold this end for a moment."

The canoe slid down, requiring Munson to reach up with one hand to prevent it from sliding down onto him. The old man took the bill—held each end in a thumb and forefinger—and popped it several times, effecting an offbeat test. Approving, he nodded and resumed unloading.

"Okay. Catch hold here."

He ordered Munson about curtly, and once again Edgar put down the shotgun within Tyrone's grasp. This time it was even harder for Tyrone to resist grabbing it. The old feeling of helplessness was growing rapidly, intensified by the fact of the worsening situation. Now, there were four people, not three.

As if realizing his error, Munson picked up the shotgun with one hand while shouldering the canoe. Tyrone and Charlie followed to the water's edge.

When they launched, the old man abruptly raised his finger, pointing at Charlie.

"But not him. Two's too many already. I charged for two,

not three."

Munson shook his head, but before he could respond, Tyrone motioned to the truck.

"Couldn't he wait there? I mean, that big grove of Spruce is only five minutes off." Then to the old man: "Couldn't he wait in your truck?"

"No, Charlie's goes with me."

The boy had returned his attentions to the river and looked back hopefully at his father.

"Dad, what sort of fish live in this part of the river?"

The old man interrupted Edgar's reply, shaking his head.

"Three people in that canoe is just doing it. Four. That's dumb. If you want, I'll take him across separate, but you've got to pay."

Munson answered the boy in his usual way, then looked at the old man, the river—then at the truck. At that moment, a pair of ravens flew over, clucking softly. Landing in the tallest nearby tree, they peered down, chortling happily in anticipation of camp scraps. Munson looked away from the pair, then gestured at the truck.

"You wait here Charlie. Your Dad will be right back, OK?"

While Munson took the boy to the truck, the old man scrutinized Tyrone from a dozen feet off, and gave a nod.

"You look beat. If these trees are close by, he could find them alone." At that point, Edgar returned, and the old man pointed critically at Tyrone. "I was just telling your partner here, he looks peaked. Can't you find these trees and this other guy by yourself?" He gestured confidently toward Edgar. "Looks to me like you're a fellow who knows his way around in the woods."

Tyrone glanced toward the truck, not liking the complexities this led to. If Tyrone stayed, would Munson then insist on taking the boy? The old man stepped closer to him, looking Tyrone frankly up and down.

"Maybe this isn't the day for you to be crossing this river."

Tyrone felt something terrible let go of him.

"No, I'm ready. Let's go."

All three men got in the canoe—the old man, who wore hip waders, steadied it while Edgar and Tyrone got in. Tyrone was amazed how stable it was, and despite the load, how lightly it squatted in the opaque water. The old man was agile, and, shoving off, he glided the canoe effortlessly onto the river.

Tyrone looked behind, watching the truck become smaller—seeing Charlie's head, just the top of it, above the dash. Beneath, he felt the swift current catch the boat, and as the old man paddled, Tyrone noted his feeling of hopelessness was gone. He felt better.

Tyrone experienced a mood of optimism, like in the old days, before his marriages, the troubles down south, and so many nights and days of hard dismal living. So many of those days had gone by, Tyrone had long ago lost count.

Everyone driving from Fairbanks stopped in at Deets' Store, which had figured so prominently in newspaper reports. At first, the Munson story went statewide, then national. Earl Deets filled his trading post notice board with clippings, and when it overflowed, he put up another. Now there was word that one of the nighttime news magazines was going to feature the whole story.

Problem was that Mrs. Munson had taken Charlie away the day it happened—just a few hours after the troopers found him wandering around on the road. The child had talked gibberish to the troopers, of course, like you'd expect. His mother had flown south to California with her son that same week and shunned all the subsequent publicity. Mrs. Munson was fiercely protective of the boy.

But the real hook to the story was that the old drunk, Tyrone, turned out to be a retired U.S. Marshall with a distinguished record. He'd somehow decoyed Edgar Munson across the river, where the lunatic had killed him, then—thank God—shot himself before he could harm others.

Just this week, Earl had gotten pretty excited about rumors of a TV movie—but those in the know told Earl that the last place Hollywood would film it was along Lost River. There would be real drama to it, though. Just the ending—Pierce, the Troopers and the dogs finding the bodies.

Pierce had secured his vest over Tyrone's face, hefted up his body, then carried it in his arms through the woods a mile and a half without a rest. Later, both troopers and the dog handler said to everyone they'd never seen such strength.

A mile and a half without a rest. Looking straight ahead. Oh, there was real drama to that ending, wherever they decided to film it.

3. Talk About Wolves

The wolves entered the Lost River drainage on a severe, windswept night when the sky was moon- and aurora-less. Each star shone as a single ancient light against absolute black. They cleared the ridge in single file, the leader in front, the remainder of the pack behind. A stiff wind curled over the same ridge as the column of hunters threaded their way into the lee of the hill—first down an open slope, disappearing into white birch.

Behind them, where they'd broken their way through fresh snow, they left a deep, jagged trail. It was not a cold winter along Lost River Drainage, and there were many snow storms with heavy, slushy snow. The pack often could not stay on top of the snow but broke through, making it difficult to hunt and even more dangerous to kill. Large prey, when they could find them, were easy to catch but wallowed desperately in snow, and avoiding their hooves was hard. In October, the pack numbered sixteen, now—in early January—only twelve. The pack held up in the birch, howling.

The next morning while skiing between Dark Creek and the divide, Pierce saw their tracks and knew there would be trouble.

• • •

An argument broke out over wolves at Deets' Roadhouse between dog mushers and some graduate students from the College.

"If they ate your collies and cocker spaniels in Fairbanks instead of our goddamned dog teams out here, you'd sing a harder line about the bastards."

Harsher words followed, and Jo Deets broke it up. Thankfully it was the students who decided to leave. The mushers and their families were regulars; the students, drop-ins.

"It was Pecky and George Roberts," she explained that

evening to Earl who remarked that he had no use for both Roberts brothers and their father Ted.

"Well," she defended, "... at least Ted works."

Earl retired to the generator shed to work on a bum compressor, for it did no good to discuss road politics with Jo, his second wife. She still had the romance of the north country in her, despite six years' residence.

"She thinks the uproad folk are somehow more *genuine* than the downroad types," he explained once again to Pierce, who, seeing him working in the shed, stopped by while hiking home.

Earl faced Pierce when he spoke, tapping a box wrench against his palm to see if his words sank home—Pierce was tolerably good at reading lips, but Earl knew it was best to speak slow and carefully.

Pierce offered his "one-cornered" smile, as his first wife used to describe it, and put his pack on the floor. He took out his corncob pipe and held it aloft, a way of asking permission to smoke.

Deets nodded and went back to work.

Pierce loaded his pipe, smoked, and in a silent way the men pondered the unwritten but steadfast social divisions along Lost River Road—the more steadily incomed people, downroad, lived closer to town, gradually giving way to part-time, seasonal and intermittent income residents farther uproad.

Uproad and *downroad* were terms all used, familiar descriptions.

Deets finished off the compressor, made a note in the maintenance record, then looked squarely at Pierce. Though he shared them infrequently, Earl had strong opinions about Lost River Road residents: "Being a musher is just a goddamned code-word for being a lay-about and letting your old lady commute to Fred Meyers or Costco for a paycheck."

Pierce's intense gray eyes danced a bit as he enjoyed Deets' jibes, the result, Pierce knew, of—in Deets' early years—being stiffed for numerous grocery and liquor tabs. The businessman motioned toward one of his rental cabins with his tool kit: "You're too damned old to be trekking around in the middle of the night, Pierce. Sleep in number six. It's done up and probably still warm."

Five years ago, Pierce would not have entertained the offer, nor would Deets have offered. Seventeen more miles to go for Pierce, even carrying a light pack, was not significant. His hiking and outdoors ability along the road were legendary.

Though the lore of Pierce's strength and durability persisted, in recent years Deets saw his increased strain with a pack: his short, robust form bent further forward, and the mute's look of relief when putting a pack down. So Pierce looked toward the cabins, thought a bit, then politely declined, motioning uproad with his pipe.

"You're a stubborn cuss, Pierce, you are. You'll die walking."

And they exchanged amiable gestures, but at the last second, Deets touched Pierce's shoulder as he was stooping to load up, looking at him directly.

"Think these wolves are the same group as seven years back? I mean, mostly?"

Pierce nodded—holding his finger and thumb apart just a bit, to gesture that at least a few of the wolves were. Deets looked uproad—as if he might see the pack crossing the road—or even coming their way. His eyes were heavy; he'd been up since before 6:00 A.M., and for the entire day all he had heard about were wolves.

"Well, I suppose they'll start in on stock and those goddamned dog teams again. I mean, that's why they're here. Damned few moose around."

Deets stopped before going inside and watched Pierce

hump the pack uproad—he still moved along without visible effort and was soon out of view. Deets took a breath, looked upward a last time at the night sky, and hoped Jo would not want to argue about the wolves. He'd heard enough for this day.

• • •

The wolves didn't hunt close to human habitation but instead hunted in the drainage northeast of Lost River Hot Springs Resort. There had been extensive clearing, and even two roads cut to facilitate work. Snowshoe hares were plentiful in the secondary that winter; better yet, in some places, there was a firm crust on the snowpack. But soon, with so many eating them, the hares became scarce. They had not been a nearly sufficient food supply for the wolves to begin with.

During the short days, the pack avoided traversing open areas, moving quickly between thickets and taller stands of white spruce, beech, and thick willows. They traveled cautiously, stopping to test the wind often, listening always. The upper reaches of Lost River—both the north and south branch drainages—were immaculate with new snow. Nowhere was there prey, and starvation traveled behind the pack—a stalker who never tired.

Early on the tenth morning—hours before the sun rose—they picked up the scent of moose and quickly found fresh broken trail. The mammoth deer could not, of course, stay atop the snow, and its trail consisted of deeply punched holes where its great legs thrust through the snow.

The wolves hesitated at the edge of an expanse of cleared river bottom where the moose had continued across. They listened, pawed the snow and sniffed, then, tossing their tails high, continued at a lope—anxious to traverse the open area.

• • •

Pierce's first experience with wolves began forty years before as a gunner in an aerial wolf-hunting enterprise. He'd been a young, eager newcomer. In the front seat of a single-engine cub, they would swoop low over the countryside and, with the door down, he'd kill the animals with pea-sized buckshot.

It was legal enterprise back then, with each pelt worth anywhere from fifty to three hundred dollars, depending on—mostly—the Asian market. There were probably over a hundred aerial wolf hunters in the state then, and there was nothing controversial about it.

"Pierce never got air-sick, and 'course the noise didn't get to him. And he *never* missed. Plus, he was a fast, expert skinner. Nary a nick or rip, that guy."

Dan Hutton, long retired, would recount his aerial-hunting days to the regulars at Deets' Café on Saturday mornings—the unofficial time of a coffee and social session for Lost River Road old-timers. At seventy-eight years of age, Hutton stood witness to changes in the northland,

"And none of the changes were for the better, goddamnit. Back then, we put a moose in the locker every fall, and," the old man would look around to check for nearby customers and, dropping his voice, conclude, "... there wasn't such a thing as fuckin' environmentalists."

Actually, Pierce avoided Deets' place on Saturday morning for precisely the reason that Hutton and others would be there. For the eight winters he worked for Hutton, the pilot and guide euchred Pierce out of his fair share in the dismal business. Of course, at the fur rendezvous, wholesalers would in turn cheat Hutton—and on it went each season.

Pierce learned about wolves, and this continued during his conventional trapping activities—his sole cash income for his first two decades. Eventually, seeing plummeting fur prices and having no interest to expand and mechanize his activities, he quit.

Years later, when times had changed, some young travelers from Norway asked Pierce, "Do you regret...this...killing of so many creatures for pelts?"

Pierce looked across the table, then wrote carefully on his tablet, slid it over, turning it right side-up for them to read,

"No. I hunted. They hunted. That's the way of things."

• • •

When the pack came across the moose, it was a behemoth bull weighing close to a ton. The creature's extraordinarily long legs, though burdened with navigating through thick snow, were skilled death-weapons close in. They found him stripping great swaths of willow bark in a thicket along the North Fork, and, fatigued from the tracking, the pack lay down in a snow-clad alder thicket, studying him. The younger pack members whined for activity, but the older ones knew this moose was out of the question.

It was full-fleshed, ill-tempered and unassailable, even in deep snow. But they watched it feed through the short, declining daylight—themselves hungry and sorely needing sustenance. Finally, unable to control their impatience, three pack members approached it when, at dark, it stopped feeding and moved into the open. Seeing the wolves—and of course knowing of their presence since midday—the irascible animal's great ears went back, and it charged down on the three, snow flying dozens of feet into the air with the phenomenal force put forth.

The three wolves scattered and returned to the pack.

They howled that night, though there was only the tiniest, most fragile sliver of a moon. At the resort, winter visitors from Germany—a group of serious cross-country skiers—listened, fascinated. Their winter holiday was now even more extraordinary.

Resident animals, though, listened with dark understanding of the hunters' primordial language. This howling was edged with more than ordinary restlessness. They listened with the certainty of things to come.

• • •

Ms. Carly's middle-school biology class stood in a semi-circle around Pierce, each holding their cross-country skis. This, she said to them, was the "second annual Mr. Pierce field trip" and laughed about that. Ms. Carly's signing was not good, and the student who'd translated the year before had moved. So a Mrs. Simons—the Dean of Girls—had volunteered at the last minute to come along. Despite being somewhat cowed by this severe woman, Pierce was impressed with the fluidity of her signing.

The day went well, and at the end he took questions about, at first, their field topic, "The World under the Snow," but they soon changed to wolves, now a hot topic. After escorting them back to the bus, he was left alone with Mrs. Simons, who'd brought her own car. She faced him, and like she had the entire day, she made him think about an *Academy of the Deaf* teacher he'd had named Mrs. Pilby. Mrs. Pilby would punish the boys by making them hold their finger on the tip of their nose for varying amounts of minutes, depending on the crime. Initially, Mrs. Simons signed questions about wolves—about if Pierce guided people out to see wolves: "My late husband and I were expert skiers, and I'm looking for an appropriate place in wolf country to distribute his ashes. Wolves to him stood for the wilderness."

Pierce replied that he did not, and he thought it an awkward notion.

At her car, he could see there was another question—while fumbling for her keys, he could see her thinking. Like Mrs. Pilby, Mrs. Simons' salt-and-pepper gray hair was gathered trimly and piled in a bun. She was a tiny woman, barely five feet, yet Pierce supposed she was like Mrs. Pilby—fierce and exacting.

She signed while fixing Pierce in her solemn, appraising look: "In the article about you, it said you hunted wolves from airplanes and had killed hundreds. Maybe more than a thousand. Was that accurate?"

"More or less."

"Can you ever make up for that, do you think?"

Pierce had never been asked about atonement, and with a glance, noticed her tiny car bore environmental activist bumper stickers, plus several organization decals in the corner of the front window. The story was done three years back—after the death of Tyrone—and he had made a point never to read it.

He became uneasy. Pierce remembered the acrimony during his first and only meeting about aerial wolf hunts a decade plus ago, and hoped she wouldn't get fierce or emotional. He signed nothing in reply, and thankfully she nodded, signed 'goodbye' and fumbled with her keys unlocking the car.

• • •

On the twelfth evening after entering Lost River Drainage, the wolves moved downroad a dozen miles, traveling parallel to it. The younger animals were uneasy, for the air was rich with bad scent, yet older members continued with strict vigilance. By the middle of the night, they held up in a thicket of willow. There was no howling or play, but instead they curled down in the snow. From almost every direction—though mostly from the south—noises made their ears constantly twitch, and only the older animals managed to doze.

At sunrise, in late morning, a southerly breeze came up, and together with unsettling scents, other, more attractive ones, accompanied them. The entire pack stood—pacing back and forth, yipping softly, and looking southward, into the wind. The wind was the hunter's intelligence gatherer, and ultimately their ally.

Even better, the temperature remained low and the skies mostly clear; instinct informed that fresh snow was unlikely. Snowfall would make everything more difficult if not out of the question.

• • •

Pierce told almost no one about his world of sounds. Though born deaf and cloaked in silence when awake, his dreams were rich with sound. They had always been a wonderful part of sleep. When he woke in the mornings, he always wondered if the sounds made by creatures and phenomena in his dream world were close to what they actually were.

During one of Tyrone's sober periods, Pierce asked him about this.

"Well, Pierce, you read a lot. So what you hear in dreams, it could be like the sounds described in writing? People describe sounds all the time. But, in the end, how things sound to others—or not—is a bunch of rot. What *you* hear is it."

And they had talked about the sounds he remembered in dreams, contrasting them with those in books, versus Tyrone's memory of sounds. These were some of their most interesting talks.

The previous night, Pierce dreamed of an owl. Throughout his sleep, it called incessantly. It was his favorite sort of owl— the tiny boreal owl. But in his bird book, it described its call differently from what he heard in dreams.

In his world, the tiny owl had a mellow hoot which carried for miles, though in the book it was described differently, not at all sonorous like he imagined. He was thinking of this during breakfast when the chef from Lost River Resort checked him out on his way to town. He had news. An excitable Finnlander, the chef talked, arms flying in every direction, while Pierce brewed tea.

"The fat's in the fire now, goddamnit. Wolves got a llama last night at twelve-mile."

The chef was a gadfly and liked controversy. Otto was in Germany, where he was most the time since remarrying and leasing the resort to Chrysler-Daimler. For once, the chef regretted his absence.

"With Otto here, that would *really* put the bee in the bonnet."

Pierce knew precisely where the killing occurred. Often, hiking by there, he fed the strange animals sugar cubes, until the owner—a professor lady from the college—gently reminded him to perhaps use carrots or grain-cakes. Pierce imagined that the animals resented being cut off from what they especially favored.

Wondering where he might go until the inevitable controversy blew over, Pierce sighed, wrote on his tablet, and slid it across to the Finnlander. The man laughed and shook his head, replying, "Oh, not me! I wouldn't miss the ruckus for anything."

The chef was so excited about his news that when he returned to his car, he found the lights had been left on and the battery was dead. They jumped it from one of Pierce's old trucks he hadn't run in over a year.

It was a cool, still morning, Pierce's favorite. The first light crept over the northern ridges of Lost River Drainage, spilling narrow shadows across the whitened landscape. It would be a good time to absent himself from the road community. Watching the chef drive off toward town, he resolved to snowshoe into the back country to his old line shack.

That spring, he planned making alder syrup again, and in addition to scouting for proper trees, he might look for a few house logs. His quasi-position as *Old Timer* would see him play sounding board to all factions, for Pierce had maintained an open-door policy. Always, he was a good host. But if he wasn't home, this would give him a smooth and graceful out.

Almost no one knew of his line shack, which was an excellent place to read and dream.

• • •

For the first time, the pack crossed Lost River Road from north to south just above the fourth bridge. In fact, after distancing themselves from the road a half mile or so, they used the frozen river itself to travel. It was only a few hours before daylight and instinct drove them, for they felt a need to put distance between themselves and the musher's dog yard. The raid was marginally successful—three of the smallish dogs yielding less-than-minimum nourishment for twelve adult wolves.

After a dozen miles, the pack recrossed the road, then traveled hard a half-dozen miles back into a stadium-like bowl formation bisected by a small stream. In the dense thickets they bedded down where they had three nights before. From the dog-yard to this shelter, they had traveled fast—taking just under an hour to reach it. There was a moonrise just a few hours before dawn, and a trio of the great beasts wrestled for a bit, then, beginning with yips and barks, began a celebratory chorus of howling.

Their voices were solitary winter spirits resonating throughout the amphitheater-like formation, traveling from the frozen willow and alder thicket along the flats, upwards. Eventually this blood-song became lost in the columnar stands of beech and dense white spruce which held burdens of snow on lush boughs that bent downward like weary, ghostly arms.

• • •

Pierce meant to leave early the day following the Finnlander's visit but became involved replacing the bindings on his snowshoes. Feeling nostalgic, he decided to snowshoe, for in recent years he'd used skis for back-country travel. More than ever, acquaintances would show up at his place with a trailer and snowmobile, and he would ride along. Pierce did not like the machines, for they stank up everything. They were fast, but what good was that to him?

Two mornings later, he was set and resolved to leave very early—he'd been lucky; so far no petitioners had stopped in. With the wolves hunting the road area, people would be trooping about with petitions to politicians and boards, or even sponsoring ballot measures.

But his resolve weakened: fresh reading material was Pierce's indulgence, but he swore not to risk a trip to Deets' prior to leaving. Yet there was also Deets' paperback swap bin. It was always full of surprises.

The temptation of nights in the line shack with fresh reading material, followed by winter sleeps and their long, seamless dreams was too much for Pierce. His gaze fell on the old truck he'd started the day before. It *did* run. Between his place at thirty-two mile and Deets' at eighteen, there would be no State Troopers, so his chronic lack of a license should not be a problem.

With the truck, the errand would take an hour.

At Deets' store, the confusion was worse than Pierce anticipated. While picking up his mail and checking out the book bin, he learned the llama had been killed by dogs—a notorious pair belonging to a dentist. However, that same night at twenty-eight mile the wolves had eaten either all or a few (depending on narrative) of the Roberts' dog team—actually, teams. The senior Roberts, not unusually, had been spending the night with their daughter in town, and their two sons were, for some reason, absent most the night.

The wolves could not have selected a more vociferous dog owner. Pierce almost made his escape before Pecky Roberts caught up with him and, virtually dragging Pierce to his truck, threw back a canvas and angrily displayed what Pierce knew would remain of the sled dogs: Just heads, completely and evenly chewed off below the collar, with bare skeletons and shreds of fur—or nothing at all—left of the bodies below. It made a ghastly visage, but typical of wolves when raiding dog yards—they almost invariably ate around any collar or linking device.

He was saved from this dismal melodrama when two dog mushers pulled up. They drove that constant musher contrivance—pickups with compartmented dog-hauling add-ons with sled carriers on top. In the excitement of their greeting and general outrage, Pierce got away.

• • •

The pack was driven by hunger and the arc of the passing sun. Now, each day was becoming longer, and as the planet tilted, the rate by which it increased became greater. Soon, mating season would be upon the pack, and the females would carry litters.

More prey was needed than what purloined sled dogs or small game could provide, and hunger was constant. Of course, a large-hoofed animal would be ideal. Yet in these new hunting grounds, there were many dangers, and none in the pack rested easily. This chronic uneasiness drove them to consider leaving—find another place. Yet the recent meal made them hesitant to abandon a known food supply, despite obstacles.

Through that day they stayed in cover, and there was little play or socializing. The older animals stayed vigilant—some napped, still experiencing a modicum of rejuvenation from the meager fare. Toward sundown, several began pacing—treading the snow flat and firm in the small runway of their pacing area.

There needed to be a decision—an action. Their basic drives of survival and hunger were pitted against one another—an old and stubborn debate that left the entire pack troubled.

• • •

Pierce's pack was heavy, and he marveled at the frailty of his memory. Skiing was easier, surely. But the snowshoes brought back the wonder of his early days in the north. He labored on at something between a lope and walk, the snowshoes keeping him securely on the crust. He'd been more sedentary than usual that winter—at 63, he wasn't as active as he once was. Oh, he walked a lot, but walking wasn't snowshoeing or skiing.

He'd just turned northeast up Dark Creek when he intersected the wolves' tracks. Pierce stooped and examined them. They had been moving fast—heading across the drainage, whereas he was ascending it.

The tracks were fresh—possibly a dozen wolves. Pierce guessed they'd passed by just prior to sunrise. This worried him—for despite regulations, locals might trail the pack on snowmobiles, and while doing so come across his fresh trail and compromise his long-treasured hermitage. Leaning into his pack, he resumed trekking, and during the next mile, the grade increased and he labored—his line shack was still a full three miles ahead.

The heaviness which settled across his chest was the first in almost six weeks: The undersides of his tongue hurt, then his throat began to tighten and ache. Pierce took off the pack and sat on it. The comings and goings of these episodes made little sense. He'd experienced the first a year ago, just sitting in his cabin.

It could be stomach upset, but more likely it was his heart. The attack continued until the heaviness was almost more than he could bear—then gradually it eased. Waiting, Pierce knew he should see a doctor, even though he lacked money or insurance—and when he was a child, he'd had his fill of doctors.

When the attack seemed over, Pierce moved on. A great demand for sleep overtook him, and more than anything, he looked forward to reaching his line shack. Working against the pack and steepness of the trail, Pierce took breathers. He looked forward to crawling into his sleeping bag and withdrawing into restful sleep. When he was a small boy, he learned sleep not only rested the body, but soothed the troubles of the previous day. And dreams created the restful sounds and language of his sleep.

• • •

The scent that came to them seemed vaguely familiar and, more than that, promising. The pack detoured from their route of the previous night, traveling directly south. Within fewer than a half-dozen miles they came across a group of paddocks.

One of the paddocks held five Shetland ponies.

The presence of these animals so confined was suspicious, suggesting dangers of traps or bait. Hunkering down, they watched and listened. Nearby was a house trailer, but it remained quiet. There were no dogs.

After an hour, they moved somewhat to the west when a light breeze came up—keeping it in their face. Between the trailer and the ponies were various items the wolves feared—the iron railings and stands for the merry-go-rounds the ponies propelled during the summer.

A favorable development was the position of the closest pony— it moved away from the others, closer to the alders. Stalking at a crawl, the pack got within twenty feet of it.

The initial attack went well. Most rushed the animal's hind end, and when the pony wheeled, two jumped the fence in front, seized its head by the muzzle and nose, weighing it down. It struggled briefly, and when it tumbled—which would be its end—it fell into the fence, collapsing it outward onto a stack of metal railings and aluminum siding. Accumulation of snow on the metal muffled the initial impact, but soon the pony's death-flailing cleared the snow and a great banging resulted. Yet the pack had drawn blood and was committed, attacking hard to stop the animal's thrashing quickly.

This commotion covered whatever warning the pack might have had, for the first three shots were expertly aimed—end-on-end—and each struck a different pack member.

The attack stopped as quickly as it began, with the surviving pack members fleeing into the willow thicket; hence the next volley was as wild as the first was accurate.

• • •

Pierce's sleep at the line shack was no disappointment. He dreamt of great times when he'd first come north. Then, his youth had held unlimited strength and stamina. Even during the coldest spells, he would suit up and start off, taking in everything—learning something new about the country each day.

And during the dream, as he moved along, winter would fall away—as if winter were only temporary clothing the country had worn resentfully. Within minutes late spring was everywhere, and this dream passage brought a silent and miraculous sweep of warmth, and more than anything, sound.

As it had so often before, his dreamscape suspended his world of silence. The late spring visitors—swallows, cranes and wedges of ducks and geese heading north—set up a peal of voices extolling the spring below, with Pierce looking up.

And there were breezes moving upriver, noisily rattling the days-old green leaves in the stands of hardwoods. These new leaves glistened with the aromatic resins of bud-out. Lost River crowded its banks with runoff, its waters opaque with the steeped sediment that blended with the dense snow melt. The current swept against the cut-banks, bending down deadfalls, eroding banks—all of it was the sound of the river coming to life.

And Pierce's own drives—like the country—would rise fully renewed. He remembered the woman. Pierce, despite the lack of snow, would ski effortlessly upriver to where she lived. By keeping curtains drawn and no light except for a tiny candle, she avoided Pierce's seeing her clearly, and, in all the rebirth of sounds, she alone remained silent.

They would quickly undress each other, and he would marvel at her strong, lean body—clearly used to hard work. Even in the near-absence of light, Pierce could tell she was no beauty—and he assumed this explained the lighting, the silence. He would penetrate her carefully, slowly. And while doing so, she would move her entire body into his, clasp her strong arms around his neck and both would contribute their own passions to the potent energy of spring.

At the conclusion—spent, holding each other in a thick quiet—Pierce would try to look fully into her face, but she would turn away. And in the end, when he would leave, she would sign slowly but clearly, "Return whenever you like."

When Pierce awoke, he experienced the descent of the old soundless curtain that held back all sounds. He peeked out from his sleeping bag and saw with pleasure his fire had just held, and the shack was not completely chilled. Struggling up, his chest hurt—residue from the attack the day before.

Before starting coffee water and going outside, Pierce began his most solemn morning ritual—he turned on his radio. It had three lights that blinked on and off with talking and music, and Pierce imagined he'd learned to distinguish between the two. The lights were a presence in his morning.

The radio was yet another trapping of civilization abandoned by Tyrone. When Pierce had asked for it, he explained how the lights interested him even though he wasn't able to hear the sound. The old lawman, somewhat in his cups, drew himself up comically, looked directly at him, and pronounced, "Pierce, you're one deranged *hombre*."

• • •

It didn't require instinct to tell the wolves their raid was a disaster. Three of them were missing—surely gone forever—and a fourth could barely keep up. She was a young female, ready to carry her first litter. One of her legs hung uselessly, and she would not be with them long.

So, there were nine now, and they had to get out—move far. Their trail was easy to follow, and the disastrous raid dictated the decision: They had to get out of Lost River drainage quickly, or before long there would be no pack. They would be hunted down and shot. The wounded female would buy them perhaps some time—enough to get over the divide and back to the vast open country where people were seldom seen.

Without much of a rest, they moved on. The desired rate of travel required risk-taking, and the pack traveled over long, open stretches. It was not quite light, though any light at all made such travel risky. In another hour or two, it would be virtual suicide with pursuit underway.

Tails high, muzzles coated in frozen vapor, their powerful shoulders thrust into each bound, they moved northeast toward the divide. The crippled female was now gone, and the pack moved on, eager to be quit of an encroachment which had yielded little prey.

• • •

Pierce considered it a joke of circumstances that for all the years he'd spent scratching for cash, it was growing all around him. Every paper birch tree, he figured, contained grocery and staple money, and for almost four decades he hadn't known it.

Old Karl Sleekside, who had owned Tok Junction Trading, revealed the potential of birch syrup: "Why, Pierce, you hardheaded fool, money's growing all around you." And he'd given Pierce instructions, and even the first year with all his mistakes Pierce did well tapping birch trees for sap. In fact, on his first payday, Pierce had sneaked the wheelchair-bound Karl out—driving him down to the Junction Pub, where they'd managed to get somewhat drunk before Karl's angry wife found him.

"Pierce—*you* of all people!"

It was still dark as he cruised the new stand of white birch—tall, reaching skyward. He followed the trunk upwards, until the beam of his light broadcasted a columnar shaft of light into the darkness above the thick grove of birch. The numerous birch stands around his line shack would yield profuse sap, and this year Pierce would move his cooking operation here. There were no better stands of birch than these in the entire Lost River drainage.

Moving from one stand to another, he again regretted not bringing skis. He remained tired and sore from the day before. The slower pace gave his mind opportunity to wander. Pierce experienced the abrupt sense of being alone—not in space, but of time—in lacking contemporaries.

Even Karl had died two years ago, and he was one of the last. Harder had been Pierce's twin sister—he learned of her death by letter. Even if he had found out sooner, he lacked the cash to fly south for the funeral. At her death, it had been six years since they'd seen each other.

Pierce struggled for air as he snowshoed, and he stopped to rest before he provoked another attack. Ordinarily, this would be an ideal respite to enjoy his pipe, but that was out. Wedging his pack against a log to make a secure seat, he sat and immediately felt the lure of sleep and thought of returning to the shack. He had stopped on the edge of a thick willow patch with a narrow but frozen creek halving it. Above, two ravens flew by, then wheeled back to see what he was up to. As they banked and came back, Pierce marveled at this effortless maneuver.

The great birds decided to rest atop a willow, and, in a comic bit of maneuvering, knocked chunks of rime from the narrow limbs as they struggled for a stable perch. He'd brought along a pack of peanuts and was considering standing and digging for them, but for the moment he was too tired. Anyway, he wasn't sure ravens were interested in peanuts. He pulled the hood up on his parka and struggled to avoid returning to his recent train of thought—about being alone.

The ravens clucked sonorously—expectantly—and Pierce knew that if he had some fish jerky, he could provide himself a show, for the great ebony rogues loved meat of any sort. The closer of the two leaned forward, its rich neck dewlap quavered and heavy bill opened as it hooted sending forth a puff of breath vapor. Its mate followed suit, and Pierce noted that the hairs at the base of their bills were coated with breath-frost, much as a mustached man might be.

At that moment—when he was watching and listening to them call—the strangeness of the situation came to him: Pierce was awake, and he could *hear* the birds. This fact startled him so, he became dazed; yet because of his dreams, these sounds were certainly not new.

The ravens became excited and swooped from their resting spots across the clearing. When Pierce followed their flight paths, he felt the familiar jolt of recognition when a pack of wolves emerged from the creekbed and moved across the clearing directly for him. The breeze blew from them to Pierce, and, without scent, they would have to see him sitting there, half concealed. They were so close he could hear their footfalls—could hear the snow crust break, and, as they bounded closer, even their breathing. In over forty years, he had never been so close to wolves.

The ravens circled, clucking vigorously—sensing that these hunters carried with them more potential for scraps than Pierce. Pierce admired the lead animal, a huge male, well over a hundred weight, each paw the size of a small dinner plate, its skull wide and powerful.

When its eyes fell upon him, Pierce imagined looking into the most basic functions of life and death; the animal's eyes shone amber, reflecting the earliest morning sun. Pierce and this beast looked at each other, and neither was alarmed or surprised.

• • •

The pack was within a fraction of a mile of leaving the Lost River drainage when they encountered an unsettling obstacle. Just after threading their way through a vast stand of white birch, they dropped down into a narrow creek. Within line-of-sight of the saddle-back exit to the drainage, they emerged anxiously from the frozen creek, intending to bound straight for this.

While crossing a small open spot, they saw the man. He was alone; they had not scented nor heard him. This lack of noise was worrisome—absolutely suspicious.

Wherever there were men, there was noise, imminent danger, or both.

They took cover and studied him. Unfortunately, the man occupied a keen ambuscade. For the pack to continue onto the saddleback unseen they would have to make a time-consuming detour.

If they could get downwind of him, scents would tell a fuller story, but what little breeze there was, the pack could not safely maneuver to leeward. So, this meant he had certainly scented them, but he had not moved. Would not move. Could not move?

The pack milled nervously; with every minute it became lighter and any pursuer would have plentiful light.

The older animals made the initial break: At the fastest pace attainable over snow, they followed the edge of the clearing, giving as wide a berth as possible to their silent observer. Hard experience taught them firearm range well before this day—and at this pace, they would be within range for only seconds. They risked this rather than further delay. As they ran, their surroundings remained harmlessly silent.

When they crested the saddleback, they did not look back but continued, beginning down the familiar slope. This would continue, as the steep contour tipped into a deep valley where a wide shallow river—now frozen—snaked along a narrow course, thick with tangles of cottonwood and alder. Eventually—miles distant, away from roads and habitations—the river fanned out, feeding an expanse of wetlands.

They were now in the watershed of this river. And to the pack, this was home.

• • •

Pierce watched as the pack hesitated, checking him out, running along the edge of the clearing, and retreating north. Pierce had never tracked wolves closely, and he decided to follow. As he began, Pierce delighted in the quiltwork of sounds emanating from all over—even that of his own breathing. The ravens, their interest increased, leapfrogged from thicket to thicket, clucking—producing a rich variety of calls that for Pierce were new and exotic.

Immediately, his tracking took on a remarkable aspect. Pierce, of course, had been easily outdistanced by the pack, but initially their tracks were fresh—and individualized, for each animal's track was its autograph. But then the tracks aged with amazing rapidity. They began the melting-out process in seconds, and in minutes were huge and almost unrecognizable, as an animal track might be after weeks of frosts and thaws. By the time he reached the saddleback—the divide between Lost River to the south, and its neighbor to the north—the tracks were virtually gone, and in fact when Pierce began his descent, there was no more snow.

The scents, feelings and sounds wove the unmistakable tapestry of spring, and when Pierce paused to survey the river and flats hundreds of feet below, the country had become gripped with the same dream world Pierce so often had visited. That he had not fallen asleep did not bother him, for he'd often suspected that one day his two worlds would join, becoming a country where the past, present, and future became insignificant.

Pierce gladly removed his snowshoes, thrust them in a pile of brush and continued. The path was narrow, and both the pack and he stuck to it as it threaded its way toward the river. Looking out, Pierce saw that spring migrants had begun arriving, and, in the expanse of wetlands below, he could see thousands of white-fronted geese—the most numerous waterfowl—spiraling in from the south. Their voices teemed a thousand lunatic chuckles and honks, and their countless wings glinted as they rose and fell in the platinum light of the sub-Arctic sun.

Pierce was only roughly familiar with this river drainage. Twice he'd tried trapping in it, but it never worked out. It seemed more rugged and less promising than the country around Lost River, even as the latter became more populated through the decades. He was not surprised to see that the first few mosquitoes were out, for with its expanse of wetlands, this side of the divide was infamously bug-ridden. In a few weeks, it would be impossible.

This was a north-flowing river. And Pierce stooped to admire the largest pack-member's perfectly outlined footprint in the soft soil when he reached its muddy bank. It was a good half foot across—and quite fresh.

When he began following the river Pierce heard the River Rat before he saw him. He was arguing with someone in some sort of disagreement—as he usually was. Deets' term for the River Rat was *raunchy*, and he hated him, resulting from an incident at his self-serve. Eventually, Deets banned him from the premises, though the troublesome old man occasionally sneaked in for something when he knew Mrs. Deets was minding the store.

When Pierce emerged from the thicket, he was treated to the closing moments of the River Rat's negotiations: He rained invectives upon two Indians who were walking away in a huff. Without looking back, one flashed an obscene gesture over his shoulder. Pierce found himself at a newly cleared haul-out—the dead-end of a narrow dirt road. Pierce of late had become out of touch with local construction plans, yet he was surprised there had not been more controversy about establishing a road to the river.

The River Rat's attentions had returned to matters under the hood of his old truck. On its door was his poorly done sign, "River Rat Cruises." He swiped at a few mosquitoes, and the moment he saw Pierce, resumed without segue his ruminating over his recent troubles.

"Pilgrims come here with their posteriors hangin' outta their britches askin' me to ferry 'em across for nothin'. *For nothin'?*" and he stared ironically at Pierce, ". . . so I tell them *'nothin' doin','* right? Ha!"

He picked up a water jug, and began to add water to the radiator. Pierce looked down at the River's edge and the canoe secured at the water's edge. At that moment Piece saw the wolves emerge from the water across the river. They struggled up the steep bank, clearly fatigued after swimming against the swift, spring current. They in turn shook off, nose to tail, in typical canine fashion. As the water flew from their thick coats, it shone in the morning sun, and for a moment each animal appeared to be surrounded by a vapory nimbus. Then, the pack set off downriver, stopping only momentarily to look across the fifty yards of water between them and Pierce. The River Rat either didn't see or didn't care about this spectacular show, being far more concerned about business.

"Well, you want to cross? It's going to cost you. No free rides. Tricky gettin' someone across in that stuff. But I know rivers. Big, medium small: I've canoed 'em all. I'm a professional."

When Pierce unzipped his coat and removed it to search his pockets, he was drenched in sweat. The air, warmed by the sun, cooled him as sure as if he'd drunk long from the purest spring water.

The River Rat watched Pierce's search expectantly, and when he saw that Pierce had found no money, shook his head sadly.

"Pierce, you're a good sort. But price is ten dollars. No exceptions."

Pierce rechecked the pockets but was not optimistic. He was nearly certain that his billfold, such as it was, was at the line shack. Also, Pierce had left his day pack where he'd first seen the wolves. Damn. Without his pack, there wasn't even the possibility of bartering with some equipment.

When he looked up, he was startled by the countenance of the old man: He appraised Pierce with something approaching a ferocity. And for the first time, he noticed the River Rat's features were ashen—not healthy—and the lines in his face were deep and clogged with tough, gray whiskers. But his eyes—topped by those great tufts of iron-gray brows—were unwavering in their intensity as they confronted Pierce's impoverished state.

The River Rat gestured toward the river.

"Maybe this isn't the day for you to be crossin' this river."

Pierce looked helplessly at the river, thought, and, during his pause, the old man ended a long appraising look, and returned his scrutiny to his radiator. Pierce felt disappointment at being unable to follow the wolves. Their tracks had been perfect. But further discussion with the peevish old man would do no good. And for Pierce to continue on this side of the river would be pointless. Pierce turned, considered using his parka for barter, but instead continued back.

• • •

Pierce regained consciousness on the floor of his line shack. He'd been made comfortable with blankets. Though he still wore his clothes, his boots had been removed and his feet were close to the tiny wood stove, wrapped in a stranger's coat. Above him sipping tea, sitting on his stool, was the diminutive Mrs. Simons from the school district. She looked him up and down with her severe, somber gray eyes. She put aside her cup and signed, "You've had a heart attack. I came across you late today while looking for a place to scatter my husband's ashes."

That made sense. His chest felt as if he'd been kicked, and it was difficult to breathe. He tried to sign, but could not—she motioned sternly for him to stay still, anticipating his questions.

"I'm alone. I put you on your parka, and dragged you here across the snow. I skied closer back to the road and used my cell phone to call for help. They'll be here at first light."

Her efforts seemed a near impossibility to Pierce, but his mind was not clear, and he tried to remember memories fresh in his consciousness, but could not. It was an old frustration, not an infrequent result of wandering the dreamworld. He could not remember going to sleep or losing consciousness, and in fact, could only remember inspecting birch trees and deciding to move his syrup operation up to the line shack. But that wasn't it—not precisely what he was trying to recall.

Pierce felt the extraordinary demand for sleep. He wanted to sign questions about how she managed, but his body was weary beyond description and sleep began to take him away. So he would again visit his dreamworld, and that much good was coming from this. Pierce never wanted to lose his ability to return to where winter nights spoke to him in the audible language of dreams.

The Bridge

Crossing the Water

"Why are you like a stranger in the land, like a traveler who stays only a night?" - Jer. 15:21

I moved to Hawaii forty-two years after I intended.

Had I done so earlier, I would have been twenty-three instead of sixty-four (and pretty much unable to walk without the help of two canes). Certainly I would have weighed a hundred pounds or so less, that extra weight being the malady that eventually crippled me.

So there is a central issue: Why did I move to Hilo, Hawaii, in the year 2005?

Prior to leaving the mainland, I heard it put in diverse ways:

What are you going to do in Hilo, Hawaii?
What in hell are you moving to Hawaii for?
How will you live out there?

And I never managed a satisfactory response, not before nor during my two-and-a-half-year residence. And not to this moment.

When I arrived on the Big Island it was early summer, getting increasingly hotter during the day, though as sunset approached, the evenings would quickly become sublime, a manifestation that lasts year round.

I managed to rent a tiny alcove in a waterfront apartment warren, a seven-story concrete blockhouse across from a rundown nine-hole golf course which boasted a matching rundown clubhouse.

The economy of Hilo had lifted off the year before, and what few things were affordable, were becoming fewer.

Perhaps I was reaching back those forty-two years and by

virtue of simple mule headedness attempting to time travel to the time when I could walk and had little or no pain in my life. And more importantly, when my attitudes were unshaped by seven years in San Francisco wino hotels, followed by a quick thirty-three years in Alaska—then amended by nine years as a failed house-owner in Washington State.

And there were the memories of a half-dozen dead friends, relatives, lovers, then wars past and present. This all was the substance that I had woven into three decades of the writing life, much of it expended on the images and people of the north.

So, there was now to be a Hawaiian coda to all this.

After a joyous reunion with my old friend on The Big Island—my 1995 Ford van waiting for me at the Hilo dock like a beloved puppy—it wasn't until a month passed that I met my second ally.

Because I'm an enthusiastic observer and interpreter of bird-sign, as bird-watching is expressed in *The Iliad* and such ancient places, I know the precise date— August 15, 2005— and the precise place—a strip of ragged lawn before a raunchy live-music and booze palace called "Shooters" on Hilo's Banyan Drive—that I first saw one.

It was an immature Pacific Golden Plover.

It was sorely bedraggled from its 2200 mile-plus flight from Alaska. Its fellow plovers during August would arrive on all the Hawaiian Islands, and out as far as Fiji, the Solomon Islands, throughout Oceania.

And the moment I saw this old friend, whom I certainly had not expected, I felt better about my unlikely presence. I suspected even then that, like the plover, I would never have a genuine home here, only a stopping place.

I had first seen them in pre-earthquake Kodiak, flying out of my path during hikes around Old Russian America. I met them a few years later as I hiked into the interior of Unalaska

Island, seeking just a few hours of peace from a 220-foot floating crab processor.

Each year, or *field season*, which in fisheries science was the vaguely Victorian term we used for springs and summers, I would see them on their nesting sites or on their way to or from them. The colorful tiny birds were with me over the years during special moments when I saw and experienced wilderness few people are privileged to visit.

These locales still populate my deep recollections, those which (thankfully) have no bounds in time and place.

On the Alaskan Peninsula, I found a mysterious land called the Ugashik Lakes, twin lakes connected by the narrowest of passages. Like so many places up north, they have a forbidding, standoffish air to them, especially in spring when the land hasn't yet flexed its full seasonal muscles.

So in the Ugashiks, during off hours from otherwise frustrating research operations, I encountered a golden plover while visiting that narrow passage between the lakes. It skittered along, *'tik-'tikked'* a bit, and immediately drew me away from its next site, feigning major wing injury.

Another decade later, to the southwest, on a lonely complex of roads I again met nesting plovers. There were hundreds of miles of residue roads—eroding, wasting reminders of World War II at the foot of the Meshik Mountains. The birds shared the eerily abandoned area where all was silent save an occasional rusted-away piece of Quonset hut banging against a crumbling frame. Around me, below me, behind me, hundreds of deserted Quonset Huts rotted into the tundra. Between them the ground was strewn with old petroleum drums. And among all this, the plovers, and other birds, nested and survived another breeding season.

They would propagate their kind, and then move south leaving us land creatures behind to deal with the winters, for me, thirty-three of them. And many of those winters were tough; not a few times I too would have left if I had such economical albeit risky means to fly.

And then, along Banyan Drive in Hilo, Hawaii, I encountered this surprise reunion—my fellow expeditionaries. Having crossed the thousands of miles of ocean, the golden plovers would fatten over the ensuing eight months, gradually donning their stark black-and-white breeding plumage. Within a few days in May, all would disappear—returning the legion of miles to their breeding grounds.

For me, I would remain on the Big Island of Hawaii through the turn of nearly a dozen seasons to witness what remained after more than two centuries of greed, plundering, and occupation. This by a society who would construct paved highways and shopping complexes in The Garden of Eden if they could locate it.

The Islanders, a golden people of diverse races, along with some of the virtual maroons remaining from the plantation days, were a residual spiritual testament to what was. Meeting these islanders made a kind of somber sense to my presence.

On that August day, the Golden Plover spoke to me with its presence, and I was able to understand. When I saw the beautiful bird, I thought about place and about movement, about time and about perspective. Standing in my own confusion, in my own meanderings and pain, I looked upon that tiny plover and saw a mentor who moved between worlds traveling on the strengths of internal mechanisms that don't provide answers, questions or reasons about the absolute uncertainty of it all.

Part II
...
The Hawaiian Island Trilogy

You do yet taste Some subtilties o' the isle, that will not let you Believe things certain. Welcome, my friends all!

Shakespeare, *The Tempest*, Act V

1. Day Tour

. . . The two prisoners were tethered tightly, their arms bound painfully behind them at the elbows.

The condemned and banished fled across South Sea oceans. Most sailed off to a slow death by want of food and water, or more mercifully, a quick death via violent typhoon. No one knew which.

It was possible they found another island, free from the wars and tribal strife they had fled.

But islanders more versed in the ways of ancient views knew there was another possible outcome: The wanderers could not only sail the seas, but also—and—especially with the most gifted of navigators—could voyage across a sea composed of not water alone but time. Exiles so skillfully piloted might find sanctuary in time and place, or possibly one but not the other.

It all depended on the navigator's understanding and reverence for the stars and the planets, and his skills at parsing their annual cycles to sail a true, redemptive course.

. . .

i.

John and Mitzi Lasser browsed the pamphlet rack of the Prince Punolawi Lodge Hotel looking for a day tour. Actually, Mitzi browsed, and John stood looking sour. Tomorrow was their "optional" day—planned to be filled with a serendipitous choice, *serendipitous* being Mitzi's word for it.

"This place is like a theme park, Mitzi. You know Polynesian Days in Chicago or something."

She had booked the Hawaiian vacation to include first four

days and three nights on Maui, then six days and five nights on the Big Island of Hawaii—the Kona Coast. Her sister maintained the latter was more "genuinely Hawaiian" than the other islands. On Maui they'd been caught in a two-and-a-half-hour traffic jam, and now another on the Big Island—yesterday for almost an hour coming in from the airport. These incidents had spun John into a bad mood. Today she promised him better things. In eighteen years of marriage, in fact, Mitzi was always the time manager of their partnership.

She picked up a pamphlet in the row marked "Day Tours." Immediately it appealed to her: *A day tour back 250 years to those days before contact with Europeans.*

She read on and John followed over her shoulder.

"At least they're making an effort."

She felt reassured by John's appraisal, then regretted it—then she reversed herself and felt reassured again.

It was the sort of muscular vacation outing they shared a fondness for, and Mitzi knew they'd found something worth their precious holiday time.

"Sort of like a South Seas Williamsburg. And certainly we're in shape and up to the hiking. "

During breakfast, she called *Ono Excursions* and booked for the next day.

• • •

They'd had to start out at 7:30 A.M. and had hurried breakfast. There were seven of them, three couples, one—the Campbells—having a fourteen-year-old daughter who was cursed with flashing stainless-steel braces across her arcade of front teeth.

John was careful to keep his voice down: "This Ford passenger van, was it here before Captain Cook?"

Mitzi never liked John's cynicism and allowed a whole-note of annoyance into her response.

"What do you want John, a canoe? It's twenty-five miles over the mountain to the trail head."

The Campbell girl—named Nancy—looked shyly out the window, doing everything possible to keep her braces from view. She never smiled, of course. Mitzi felt sorry for her, for she'd worn braces once. Since both Nancy's mother and her daughter had brilliant, auburn hair, Mitzi thought to build up a bit of sisterhood and remarked how striking this mother-daughter genetic blessing was to Mrs. Campbell. In response, the young girl looked at Mitzi mutely, grinning a bit blandly— as if Mitzi had asked the time in Hungarian or Estonian. She caught the trace of a smirk from John who feigned interest looking out the van window.

Feeling somewhat awkward, she resolved to say little more to them—at least in initiating talk.

The tour guide and driver was Vera Uhane but, despite the name, she didn't look Hawaiian. Or Asian. She described the countryside as they went. Finally, there was a couple from Seattle—the Skeeters—who asked frequent questions, and that was good, for John and Mitzi along with the Campbells were a good audience.

Driving from the leeward to windward side of the island of Hawaii, one could observe the vegetation change rapidly from the arid, almost desert-like terrain of the Kona side to thick jungle, with massive gorges, or *palis*, so steep that, according to the guide, between the eras of the missionaries and sugar plantations until the use of stout gas-powered vehicles, they were only passable by mule and horse, and then only by local animals familiar with each *pali*. The driver laughed. She had a way of pointing straight up, and circling her index finger in rhythm to her talk.

"In those days, a mule from out-of-town, so to speak, wouldn't even think of going up and down an unfamiliar *pali*."

Before them the two-lane highway opened, and ahead the sea rolled from the northeast, green and without end. The horizon was straight, sharp-edged, like a ruler. The driver's hand went up; the little circles in the air became wider, perhaps to emphasize the vastness of her words.

"There's nothing out that way, folks, but Mexico, 2,400 miles off."

Mr. Skeeters wore a peculiar look—squinting out to sea, as if he might be able to see cabanas and seaside cantinas if he looked long enough.

They turned off the highway, and at once the road narrowed and began a long series of descending switch-backs. There was no traffic and Vera Uhane concentrated, becoming serious with the job of driving.

Quite abruptly, on the road ahead, a woman stood, holding up her hand. Their driver seemed relieved.

"Oh, here we are."

Their greeter stepped to the side and talked with the driver, and for the first time the clients heard the Hawaiian language spoken rapidly and with ease.

"Sounds strange, doesn't it?"

Their fluency impressed even John. Vera Uhane stood up, stooping somewhat in the van, and gestured outside—a flourish. Her cheerful mood had returned.

"Nalihina will take you from here, and I'll pick you back up sharp at 6:00 P.M. Aloha and mahalo from all of us at *Ono Excursions*."

Nalihina, a bubbly young woman who had classic Hawaiian features, asked them to double-check their footwear, even though she traveled barefooted.

"She looks like an illustration in *Typee*."

John ran the business office at the same community college where Mitzi taught literature—authors and poets were not his strong points. Mitzi, smiled, and corrected him,

"I don't know to which illustration you refer, Dear, but Melville's *Typee* took place in the Marquesas."

"Close enough. Well, here we go."

In fact, Nalihina was very attractively barefooted. And Mitzi noticed with irony that the three men, and certainly John, at once became more interested in the day's events. Starting off into a *pali,* which dropped so precipitously that the descent seemed vertical, Mitzi looked at an uneasy young Nancy whose mouth was shut so tight it became a fish-like pucker.

They held their arms out in front of them, palms down, as if to grip the handle of an imaginary ski-lift.

• • •

Halfway up the second *pali,* the Campbells began to fear for the steepness.

"Do you think we'll be all right?"

They glanced worriedly at Nancy, who swatted at the not-inconsiderable numbers of mosquitoes and looked to her parents, shrugging. She was young and, despite her parents' concern, seemed unfazed by the effort.

But it *was* steep.

The trail down was cut—incised—into the side of the hillside—more a cliffside. Though crushed rock had been put down for a treadway, it was still somewhat muddy. At once, Mitzi could see the practicality of bare feet, for Nalihina walked along seemingly without effort, her feet meeting the earth securely. No sliding or slipping with them. Everyone sweated, and, as the morning wore on, the temperature rose incrementally with the sun's ascent.

Then within a quarter hour the sun became shrouded with thick clouds, and the rain forest grew to an eerie half-dark. Nalihina turned and looked down the gorge toward the ocean.

"Oh, we have a real show coming our way. We best stay here and watch."

They looked seaward. At this point the *pali* was very narrow, but as it extended funnel-style toward the sea, it became wider. It was like they occupied the upper, narrower portion of a tree-lined cornucopia.

Seaward it seemed nature itself became suddenly possessed with a need to demonstrate how it alone decided the fate of these islands. The clouds stirred inside themselves while moving steadily toward them. From their bases, sheets of thick, dark grey rain—Biblical deluges of water—swept down earthward. The sea beneath became stippled, and with darkening of the overcast, turned into a rising then subsiding creature composed of angry grey water.

This wall of rain beneath the clouds fell with such a force while traveling toward them that it was unsettling. The excursion clients who'd initially looked at this onslaught with curiosity became anxious. Mrs. Skeeters' voice was a mixture of awe and fear.

"Oh, my goodness!"

She leaned into her husband, and Nalihini raised her hand and ordered, "Listen! It is *wai*, the coming of water."

The invincible rains pelted the rich greenery of the thick forest in the *pali* with a sudden violence. So vast a tonnage of rainwater fell, the sound was that of a virtual tornado-wind, growing more menacing as it advanced.

Deafened, Nancy Campbell and her parents covered their ears, and Mitzi and John hugged while the wall of rains advanced.

As this aqueous force came within a quarter mile, the banana trees—and there were hundreds of them that choked the steep sides of the landscape—began to thrash, along with all the vegetation: The trees, their limbs—also the massive elephant ear plants, the stands of giant bamboo, the old, gnarled trees with ground ivy growing over almost every inch of them—all of this vegetation was beaten downward, stooping and gyrating from the force of falling rain.

Mitzi resisted an urge to bolt when the wall was only yards away—advancing precisely as if they were standing in the path of an ocean breaker speeding onto a beach.

"Watch out, kiddo!"

John hugged her even closer when the wall engulfed them. They stepped back under a rocky overhang that itself was thick with a stand of ferns, and though they still got wet, it did something—perhaps, Mitzi thought, saved them from drowning!

"My God. Like a freight train!"

And like a speeding train, it passed by them in less than five minutes.

In the aftermath, water ran off in gallons from everything—all the vegetation—sending rivulets and copious runoff dozens of feet down into the forest. The sound became a staccato symphony of the percussive, and the Campbell girl looked overhead and proclaimed, "Awesome," and only for the tiniest of seconds exposed the dreaded braces. She closed her mouth back up, looking furtively left and right: Had anybody seen? Looking seaward, Mitzi and John were relieved that no more of these watery tumults were headed their way.

"Aloha from the rainy side of our Big Island of Hawaii."

Nalihini laughed, and started back up the steep incline, and Mitzi—following directly behind her—noticed with envy how attractively she moved, how effortlessly her legs and hips struck the rhythm of her uphill climb.

They all ascended in silence.

The young Campbell girl looked down, concentrating on her climb. Mrs. Skeeters, a somewhat doughy looking woman who Mitzi estimated took poor care of herself, endured the climb with difficulty. John, who really was a gentleman always, helped her when a particularly difficult portion of the trail confronted them.

In a moment when Mitzi and John exchanged a private look, she noted it was a good look, and felt he was now completely behind the decision to spend the day experiencing the village.

ii.
The elderly couple wandered the island, he muttering nonsense and she leading him. He only managed an occasional lucid moment each day and always asked the same question: "What has happened?"

"I don't know."

Each time, she answered the same way. She was patient, and her response was always kindly and a little apologetic. And, it was the truth, for she did not know.

• • •

When they broached the top of the *pali*, the trail turned seaward. They now hiked a gentle downhill narrow shoulder along the deep, lushly greened gorge.

Mitzi was grateful that Nalihini took the time to explain the different varieties of plants—flowering native trees. Mitzi was tiring, and checking her wristwatch, noted they'd been hiking almost three hours.

The moment she removed the water bottle from her pack an odd sensation of weightiness spread across her shoulders. It became such a burden that, despite the nearby volcanic slab being somewhat muddy, she sat, making only a cursory attempt to clean it. John felt it too.

"Jesus. Feels like a lead weight, doesn't it."

He sat beside her; using the tail of his t-shirt, he wiped his face, now beaded with sweat that refused to evaporate. They all felt it, and Nalihini called for them to drink more water,

"After such a rain during the day—you know, right after it clears up," she gestured up at the now nearly cloudless sky,

"... the air becomes essentially sodden with moisture. If you're not used to it, *stifling* is a good word for it. Let's all take a good fifteen-minute break. We can use it."

"Well, it *is* a bit humid."

Mr. Skeeters sat next to his wife who'd rested at the first opportunity. If there was a sensation closest to what Mitzi felt, it was the same as when they'd sauna'd at a neighbor's house: like those occasions, the vaporous heat was so oppressive it brought her nearly to the point of passing out.

Mr. Campbell swiped at his brow, but it was futile; he'd become covered with beads of sweat, and his clothes clung. He tried a smile, but it was hard.

"Man, I've never felt *anything* like this."

His wife made quite a sour face, swiping away with annoyance at sodden strands of her auburn hair.

"Weird. I don't like it."

Nalihini remained buoyant.

"It'll pass. I'll say an island prayer for a proper breeze."

Mitzi rested against John, overwhelmed by this palpable weight. Perhaps it was this that brought a spell of drowsiness—actually, she was certain it was the cause. John rested his chin atop her head, and she could sense from his chest, that he too was close to napping.

It was a feeling of intimacy they had not shared in some time and despite this oppressive vapor and heat, Mitzi enjoyed the moment. When she opened her eyes, Nalihini was standing looking toward the ocean. She held up both arms, palms out, as if to greet the breeze she was trying to summon.

"Oh, here it comes," she said. "A gift from the sea."

And indeed, a subtle breeze arrived, graciously soothing. Beyond the swaying crowns of the coconut palms the turquoise blue seawater shattered against the jagged shoreline. The sight was a balm almost equal to the breeze. The long-trunked trees swayed to the trade winds and this tableau enchanted. Mitzi experienced a fantasia: might this bit of time sustain itself in all ways, remaining fixed in memory forever? She felt enraptured, then at once, a little silly.

They all welcomed this increase in the breeze. Mr. Skeeter yawned, and his wife managed, "Oh, that *is* nice." Mitzi sat up, and John followed, blinking as he always did when waking from a cat-nap. Mr. Campbell did a rapid shake of his head.

"Jesus, talk about a wet blanket."

Each of the Campbells seemed somewhat logy, perhaps they too had napped. Mitzi felt refreshed from both the breeze and the rest.

Seeing her wards rested, Nalihini began what sounded like an oft-recited list in preparation for their arrival at Kahiko Village.

"*Kahiko* means old in Hawaiian, as in ancient. And the villagers follow strictly the practices of the *Kapu* system, for this makes the *Ono Excursions* experience genuine. It is an unprecedented look back in time. So. And with this "*going back in time*" theme, no one in the village will 'see' you or react. They'll do so only with me, and of course, speaking in Hawaiian," and she smiled, bowing slightly, ". . . and *I'll translate*. When you have questions, ask me. If I don't know, then I'll ask a villager. And," she drew a breath, and smiled, and Mitzi detected something forced in it, ". . . if you see me do something, follow suit, because it will be the custom. And customs in ancient Hawaiian Society are rigid and central to everything. I'll fill you in as we go along, of course. I will say when pictures and such are allowed, for in some areas, taking an image, or even attempting to do so, will outrage the nature of *Kapu*, and we mustn't do that. So, if you have doubts—just ask me. Now, all stay together. We're close to the village."

The path was now well used and neatly maintained, some of it with fine pebble treadway. After another quarter-mile it was bordered with round, uniform-shaped rocks with bright whitewash.

Mitzi read about the *Kapu* system the previous night on the internet. John feigned disapproval of her computer efforts—*("Wasn't a vacation supposed to be free of such trappings as computers and time schedules?")* Yet Mitzi's notebook computer was now an irreplaceable travel companion.

In fact, the computer and its unstoppable efficiency was a point of mock contention between them. Yet John politely set his book aside and listened while she recited various facts.

Mitzi felt her efforts put her at something of an advantage, although the scramble of Hawaiian and Polynesian terms didn't seem to stick in her memory like English terms might.

At the perimeter of the village, John's hand came up, taking her gently by the shoulder.

"I'll bet you a back massage that I'll be the first to see more than five post-contact items?"

He pointed to his right eye alluding to his expertise at picking up on detail.

And it galled Mitzi that he didn't have long to wait. In just a few hundred feet they passed a collection of tiny hovels—not so much constructed as tossed together ineptly—and before it sat three people. Caucasians. Two were ancient, the third somewhat less so. They sat amidst coconut and shellfish middens, and the wind for the first and only time picked up the stench of human habitation. The three were bothered by flies, and the two eldest trailed long tresses of grey hair, while the one woman—somewhat younger—had noticeably rust-tinted hair, which at one time, Mitzi guessed, had been red or auburn. The trio were unkempt and pathetic, yet something nagged at her, for they seemed strangely familiar.

"My *God*, who are they?"

Nalihini hardly paused to notice them, and looked at Mrs.

Campbell politely and shrugged, "Oh, drifters. Not Hawaiian people. *Homeless* you call them on the mainland, right? They attach themselves to those who have the skills to gather food. The Islands are tolerant of them, even here."

Their appearance was so wretched that John didn't mention the immediate confirmation of his anticipated sighting. They moved on, anxious to get the unfortunates behind them.

When they began to encounter village structures, they were different from anything she'd seen, and they immediately began drawing comments from the *Ono Tour* group, especially Mr. Skeeters who seemed to be into the construction trades.

They strolled, Nalihini commenting in depth as they encountered each different structure, explaining how they were built, of what material, establishing expertise and an impressive ability to communicate it.

At first there seemed to be no people. Then a few appeared from inside the houses. This village's adherence to tradition extended to the women not wearing tops. At first this seemed overdoing things to Mitzi, and she could see Mrs. Campbell and Mrs. Skeeter, looking at their husbands, and Mrs. Skeeter playfully backhanded her husband for a comment Mitzi hadn't caught. John, who prided himself at conducting himself with composure, appeared unfazed by this detail of genuineness.

Initially, even Nalihini went unnoticed or ignored by villagers; then she held a long conversation with one, a tall lavishly tattooed man. Her clients, as she'd predicted, seemed invisible to all the villagers.

Nalihini seemed unsure after the long conversation, and looked after the man as he walked away. Finally, as if deciding the issue, she turned, and explained, "There's going to be a *ceremony,* of sorts. And Nahua is going to see if we can watch. Sort of a hearing. A religious hearing. If we do, we'll only see a portion of it. "Suddenly she brightened. "But first, lunch! Ancient style."

And they *were* hungry. They moved deeper into the village, which contrary to Mitzi's concept of a South Pacific village was not arranged casually, but instead highly ordered, with small pathways and even what might be construed as narrow streets.

Structures and out-structures were in line, arranged by size and social standing of the occupants—some very large, and entirely open ended, while others were smaller, with a slat-ribbed opening at the end. Through these apertures Mitzi saw villagers going about their activities.

"The women will eat in here," and Nalihini pointed into a modest structure; then turning left, she indicated a much larger one, "... and the men in that."

And on cue, the man she called Nahua appeared, nodded—the first anyone other than Nalihini had acknowledged them. He gestured toward the men's eating house. Though Mrs. Skeeter and Mitzi had begun to follow Nalihini, and Mr. Skeeter, Nahua, the others hesitated, and Nalihini explained, "It is the core of the *Kapu* system that the genders never eat together. This is very much a part of our complete experience."

Mitzi, in a sudden seizure of kittenishness, stuck her tongue out at John as each group moved off to lunch. Mrs. Skeeters noticed, and gave her a brief sisterly squeeze on the forearm.

"So, Mrs. Lasser, you did some homework, I see. You knew about the Kapu on eating?"

And they shared a laugh as they entered for lunch.

• • •

After lunch they resumed the tour by inspecting the system of carefully irrigated taro patches along both sides of the stream. Taro was the primary source of nourishment for the village. In fact both women and men had been treated to *poi* during mealtime. Nalihini stooped, and touched one of the plants.

"Taro patches are the centerpiece of a Hawaiian community."

A steady drumbeat began, a single, deep-throated drum. Nalihini turned to acknowledge the arriving Nahua. She exchanged a few words with him, and he walked away with great purpose. For a moment, Nalihini seemed uncertain how to begin, then explained, holding her index finger aloft, to indicate the drum.

"That signals the beginning of the ceremony." She moved in front of them, gestured for all to gather around. She became serious—clasping her hands together into a prayer-like wedge, and dipping them in time to her words for special emphasis.

"Now, this process we are going to witness is one of ancient Hawaiian justice. Today's tour has a special surprise, for the village moves back and forth in time, in a manner of speaking. The ancient Hawaiians believed in...," she thought for a moment for the appropriate words, "...well, in English it could be termed *time sailing*, or *drifting*. They believed that time had the same potential, voyage-wise, as the ocean. So, today, I'm told, we've sailed to the year 1779, and the year *following* the arrival of Cook's two ships. So, we're here at an especially informative moment. Now, just follow me, and do as I do. I'll explain as we go along, though we must be especially sensitive to Kapua. So watch me."

Unlike before, villagers came out from everywhere, including children. The tour group, Nalihini leading, fell into line with these, who, like all villagers, ignored their presence.

"So *hokus pokus* and *shazam*, that ends the pre-contact era for *Ono Excursions*." John drew very close to Mitzi, and almost whispered his snippet of sarcasm. She again resented it.

"*Some* people respect other peoples' myths, John."

She allowed bite into her words and regretted it when he rolled his eyes and formed a wordless '*ouch.*' She drew away from him somewhat. Within minutes, they came to a nearly tennis court- sized house woven and supported with wood-pole framing. Arrayed before it were two semi-circles of garish feather standards, dominated with plumages that were a deep iridescent crimson. Other colors and materials blended in to form what Mitzi assumed were totemic designs.

This imposing array formed a semi-circle around this house, and Nalihini cautiously beckoned them somewhat aside of the group, then in hushed tones informed,

"This is the *hale ali*, the house of the high chief. And...."

She became at once silent, for emerging from it, carried on a litter was the high chief himself, an elderly, wizened man who at one time, Mitzi guessed, must have been huge and powerfully muscled. At once all bowed to the ground, going to their knees, then even more remarkably, flat on their faces. Immediately Nalihini did, too. The first to follow her lead were the Skeeters, Mr. Skeeter clearly uncomfortable on his knees. Mitzi quickly followed, as did John with an audible sigh—one of his familiar *my bountiful patience* sighs.

But the Campbells were slow to kneel, and when they did, they stayed upright, not lying face down in the acrid-smelling sand and earth. Mitzi peeked at them and saw Mr. Campbell take everything in with a sardonic smile; his wife and daughter, like him, remained upright.

The drumming increased—or actually, was joined by three other drummers who were on the left side of the Chief's House. Nalihini resumed a kneeling position. She looked back at the Campbells—motioning them down when the captives were brought on.

The two prisoners were tethered tightly, their arms bound painfully behind them at the elbows. Their escorts were four massive sentinels carrying richly designed cudgels. The drama was enhanced immeasurably by makeup so skillful it was abundantly believable, reminding Mitzi of her summer internship years ago at a Hollywood studio. Of all the movie and television people, makeup people's artistry left the greatest impression with her.

"Jesus, look at those fucking shillelaghs."

John had allowed that to escape, thankfully close to Mitzi and *sotto voce*. Mitzi saw their tour companions—all were now upright on their knees—also eyeing the massive cudgels carried by the warriors. The prisoners were barely conscious, pathetically emaciated, and wore distinguishable tatters of 18th-century-type jerseys and trousers, though without shoes. They were covered with cuts and abrasions, and one's eye was hideously rendered to appear gouged out, and terribly infected.

When the Chief raised his hand very slightly—as if it were almost too much of an effort—the drumming stopped at once. He looked at the prisoners impassively. In the minutes following the cessation of the drumming, everything around them became especially silent.

Sounds beyond the village dominated.

The surf broke with steady insistence, but even this did not intrude upon the Chief's deep, thoughtful mood. His virtual reverie carried on until emerging single file round the corner of the chief's house came a priestly procession: At its head and rear were two more warriors carrying similar cudgels, and between them were three shaman. No one looked or took note of their arrival. Mitzi was repelled somewhat when one of the prisoners coughed up what appeared to be bloody mucous, his shoulders—emaciated anyway—pinching together in the effort. One of the tour group uttered an audible '*ooooh*' of repugnance, but she didn't see who. The priests joined the Chief in the silent contemplation of the two sailors.

At that moment, the second prisoner stirred, and looked up—tried to say something, but was forced violently to the ground by one of the warriors who brought his muscular leg and foot down upon his back so violently the prisoner's head struck the earth with a distinct and sickening report—audible to all. All the *Ono Excursion* members gasped, and Nalihini whispered almost inaudibly, looking with uncharacteristic anger toward her wards, "Please. Silence. No one speak."

Or was her look not of anger, but terror? Mitzi was parsing between *terror* and *anger* when the Chief gestured, the drumming resumed, and the warriors dragged the prisoners off. At that precise instant the prisoner with only one eye saw them, his remaining eye fixed precisely on Mitzi. At once, he did recognize the visitors' presence, doing so by raising his hand and appealing with words she could not understand.

As before, this infraction brought retribution: The nearest warrior seized him by his tethers, but he lunged forward, and in that fraction of time before they could pull him back to the ground, he looked wildly toward them and this time his pathetic outcry was understandable. It was not only in English, but each word rang with unmistakable clarity: "*Oh, Jesus Forgive me!*"

And then they were gone, the priests following last.

Mitzi found herself stupefied by this extraordinary show—she could not have spoken if she tried.

Then events went wrong so quickly their sequence became obscured by the ensuing uproar.

She was certain the unraveling began when Nancy Campbell stood while reaching down for her waist pack, and this drew Mitzi's eyes away from the Chief's House. She saw the girl unbutton one of the pack's pouches and begin to remove what might have been her camera. Mrs. Campbell reached out—was it to prevent her from getting a camera? Mitzi hadn't decided what she meant, when she heard Mr. Skeeter shout with great indignity: "*This is an outrage! One thing this gore, but this! In front of our women!! I've paid good money for this!*"

Mitzi turned and saw the Chief's cape being held aside by

two attendants, fully exposing him. He urinated copiously into a gourd held by one of them, and Mr. Skeeter was on his feet, pointing at him—venting his indignation on Nalihini.

Their guide hadn't really reacted, save for her mouth to drop open, but without hesitation or gesture from anyone, Mr. Skeeter was seized by two warriors who pitched him headlong to the ground. One drew back his heinous club when Mrs. Skeeters threw herself on him, grabbing his arm. Behind Mitzi came the sound of more violent action: Nancy Campbell had also been seized by a pair of warriors. She screamed, and John cried, "Let her go, goddamnit!"

They dragged her away from John's outstretched hands, sliding her between them in the dirt; her camera—for indeed it was that she had reached for— came loose, rolling away. Two warriors, those who initially had guarded the prisoners, reappeared with just one of the priests, re-emerging from behind the Chief's lodge. The lone priest carried a large stone bowl of bloody remains. Protruding from it was a skull—its soaked hair protruding in abject and sickening disarray.

Mitzi remembered no more, save a last moment when she fell backwards against somebody—whom precisely, she did not know. In the instant before she blacked out she recalled one thing—a sense of gratitude for seeing no more.

iii.

The years of wandering made the couple expert nomads. They traveled from good place to good place, for even in these tropical islands, there was definitely a rhythm of summer and winter. Some areas abounded in numerous tropical fruits, others in brilliantly colored fish easily caught in streams. Some locales were different, rainless, even desolate, yet with complex systems of volcanic warm ponds, and even one with flowing lava—and there they enjoyed fire.

At night over the fire he would look vacantly into the embers, and before curling together and sleeping, he would ask, "What has happened?"

"I don't know, dear."

The old woman wrapped her arm around him, stroking him gently over his head, feeling the old, deep scar under his thinning white hair.

• • •

Mitzi regained consciousness to the incoherent outcries of Nancy Campbell. Her parents tried vainly to control her. Next to them—sprawled on the ground—were the Skeeters; he very muddy, visibly shaken, and clutching his wife to him. She held him too, swaying, her sobs muted, more a series of slow sniffles. John's voice had an unusual firmness to it: "Calm her down. Be easy!"

Mitzi struggled, discovering she was fighting against John who clutched her firmly. When she realized she was safe against him, she looked out at the Campbells who tackled their daughter when she suddenly jumped up with the possible intent of bolting off the side of the gorge into the tangle of trees and forest below. Mrs. Campbell managed to catch her by the right calf, while Mr. Campbell jumped up, took her by the shoulders, and struggled against blows their daughter began to rain upon them—first to her mother below, then on her father behind her. The frantic girl's auburn hair thrashed, strands of it adhering to her face; her mouth, fully open, spewed animal-like outcries.

"Nancy! It's straight down. You'll die."

Mitzi, seeing this familiar steepness, realized they had somehow moved, or been moved, back to the area where earlier they'd rested with Nalihini after the rainstorm. Above her, John continued to instruct the frantic Campbells to try and lay their daughter down.

"She's in a state of hysteria. I'll be right there."

During the Kuwait War, John had been a medic, and in fact, for almost his entire tour there, he was one of the few assigned to attend the thousands of hapless Iraqi POWs. He was a good medic, something few knew about his military background. He slid back into that role effortlessly.

John returned his gaze to Mitzi: "You okay, kid?"

Mitzi nodded, and he let her go, quickly taking off his shirt and putting it around her.

She drew in the shirt, for despite the temperature, she felt cold, and in fact began to tremble. Or had she been trembling?

From the experience perhaps? My God! Why not? For in a flash of recollection, she remembered events in the village.

She looked around, but there was no Nalihini. Mitzi reasoned a good half mile separated them from the village. She was reassured, but only for a moment.

"Shouldn't we go at once?"

The Skeeters had collected themselves; Mrs. Skeeter nodded vigorously, but instead Mr. Skeeter faced the Campbells. The girl's screams were those of someone no longer reacting to anything around them but terror internalized. Her outcries rose and fell, a siren-like monotone.

"Can't you quiet her? They'll hear. Something more awful will happen. We're going."

Struggling, John and Mr. Campbell somehow wrestled the young girl back to the ground. While in the process of keeping her down, John looked at Mr. Skeeter, saying very evenly, despite the screaming, "Going where? You don't think there'll be someone at the road waiting for us at six o'clock with gift baskets or some such, do you? I'd just sit and collect yourselves."

When John reached for his waist pack, its absence caused

him to exclaim its absence out loud and then everyone, save the unfortunate Nancy Campbell, realized their belongings too had been removed.

"And my travel pouch."

"My God! And mine! It was...."

Mrs. Skeeter stopped short of saying precisely where her pouch had been, but her shocked features made guessing unnecessary.

"Oh, for God's sakes. We've been robbed as well."

Mitzi rose, and spotted the jumble of their possessions in the middle of the trail: day and waistpacks were all thrown together along with travel pouches, water bottles and the plastic contents of wallets and security pouches. In the muddy walkway money and travelers checks lay badly soiled, several torn.

"There they are."

Stepping that way, Mitzi was marveling at the money, travelers checks and credit cards so discarded, when she saw the equally strange but neat pile formed from their electronic devices: Cell phones, cameras, I-pods, and such were neatly cracked open—like one would crack nuts or small coconuts, and meticulously sorted through.

In what must have been lengthy and uncannily detailed work, the only parts remaining in any of the electronics were plastic or synthetics.

By the time Nancy Campbell had been subdued and her outcries reduced to weeping, they all determined this strange purloining held true for everything: All metal had been taken from their belongings and bodies, including rings, a necklace from Mrs. Skeeter and even the pin through Nancy Campbell's belly button. All spare change was gone, and in the final remarkable revelation, after she lay still enough for inspection, the Campbells spotted blood at the edge of their daughter's mouth. When they looked closely, they discovered that her stainless-steel brace-work had also been removed.

"I'm getting the hell out of here and fetch the police while there's still light."

Mr. and Mrs. Skeeter were up and gone—going the direction they'd come from the van.

"I guess we should go, too."

Mrs. Campbell said that without conviction, for Nancy appeared not up to anything, and the former cast a dejected look after the Skeeters. John checked his wristwatch before realizing it was gone, then shrugged. "I make it to be only minutes before sundown. It happens fast here—at this latitude." He looked up trail, forming his mouth into a disapproving scowl. "They should have stayed put. Flight responses are trouble."

Mitzi could see John was right. In the jungle of the *pali* shadows grew lengthier, and everything was receding into soft shadows. Through the thick trunks of the trees the lingering daylight became less with each minute, and save for the sea in the distance, there was silence.

She stood, testing each leg.

"Do you think they drugged us at lunch?"

"Had to. No other way."

Mr. Campbell replied while looking blankly toward the village, then back at daughter and wife. The girl, thankfully, was almost silent, with her mother close, holding her, and stoking the girl's head evenly.

Drawing close to Mitzi, John whispered, "I gave her a seasick pill. That did it."

He sat and sorted through the remains of their packs, and without being told Mitzi knew his "survival" pocket was John's focus. He slumped, shook his head and muttered, "Afraid of that. Damned match container was metal."

"Matches?"

"None. Gone."

They sat together watching the Campbell family. It was now almost dark in the tangled vegetation of the gorge, and

John held a plastic bottle of mosquito repellant in front of them, a gesture that meant all was not lost.

In the trees they heard a breezy sigh, and then the rise of a light wind as it wove through the leaves and branches. And at the very cusp of dark, Mitzi could see the tops of the coconut palms swaying in time to the wind, a pilgrim from the open sea.

• • •

The rains began just after dark. It was a moonless night, and the clouds blotted out the stars, and if during the day there was drama to the sweeping, tropical rains, they became alarmingly moreso at night. The sounds of the massive sheets of rain tumbling into the trees and undergrowth rose and subsided with each passing weather front. The lull between deluges was marked with staccato runoff from countless leaves, limbs, and thick overhangs of vines.

Mitzi and John held each other; with darkness all visuals ceased. They could no longer see the Campbells or in fact hear them. The path—only two feet in front of them—was equally invisible with this most unsettling darkest of nights. During the intervals between downpours, Mitzi thought she could hear the sounds of water running off down the path—the rippling sound of fast-flowing water.

They huddled through the night, saying nothing to each other, getting as far back in the tiny alcove in the *pali* as they had during the day when Nalihini watched over them. The vigor of the falling rains, as before, stirred the air, circulating the pungent smells of vegetation, both fresh and decaying. In the confusion of the night, the smells brought back memories of Mitzi's mother bringing her to the neighborhood nursery each early spring prior to gardening time.

She'd enjoyed those smells, but not now.

Perhaps several hours before dawn she must have slept—perhaps they both did—for when she woke, they were huddled even closer, not only for each other's comfort, but against a surprising chill. In fact, John, always slender, began to tremble. Then—with the most frail of outlines—hints of light came from the east.

And while the first moments of sunlight increased, a rich polyphony of birdsong commenced—far more noticeable outdoors, of course, even in the muted thickness of the lush gorge. In this first light, Mitzi saw that the Campbells were not there.

"Where in earth have they gone?!"

Her long-silenced voice was an embarrassing croak, and John too struggled to find voice before managing,

"Walked off in the dark? They didn't seem the sort. Not with a hysterical girl."

In fact, the pile of looted electronics was gone, and more amazingly the pathway's presence was only hinted, if that.

"Can jungle grow that fast?"

"Evidently. We'd better get out of this gorge. Road is that way."

Both urgently desired the safety of the inn. They knew that whatever degree of crime or hoax was visited on them by the wrongdoers of *Ono Excursions*, they were on their own out here.

Unlike the others they would not panic. In fact, Mitzi and especially John were hardy trekkers, comfortable with their abilities. They labored down into the *pali*, threading their way along the more or less overgrown pathway. John picked up a stout branch and fashioned it into a beater. Working somewhat ahead of her, he cleared portions of overgrowth away as they made their way along—far slower than the day before.

In the deep, shadowed "V" of the gorge, the tiny stream, its course strewn with chunks of lava, had swollen in size and volume. It flowed noisily toward the sea; in fact this was the watercourse that served the village, irrigating their taro patches and providing it with the precious runoff.

Ascending the other side of this great geological gash into the mountainside, became hand-over-hand work, and through the morning both climbed, then descended without talk, intent on returning to the road.

Late in the morning, with the sun very close to its highest point, they shared the last of their water from the plastic water bottle, and looked out on the upswept verdant flank of the great mountain.

"We've missed the road somehow. I think they moved us somewhere that wasn't on the trail, away from the place we were dropped off. Maybe *far* away."

At the top, after emerging from another deep gorge, they realized that they either missed the road or had not begun their trek where they thought they'd been. Or something of each.

They took a long rest, and John refilled both plastic water bottles. He looked once again—and fruitlessly—for the water purification pills. Carried in a glass bottle, they too had been purloined, but they were thirsty and drank deeply. To the east the ocean stretched as before, blue and vast, the oncoming ocean swells cruising in languourously from the northeast.

John guessed it to be precisely midday, and Mitzi knew she was about to hear a male-decision, for John always had an amusing way of holding himself, of glancing quickly in numerous directions—like a robin on their lawn— when arriving at a serious declaration.

"With those two volcanic nobs over there," he gestured a few hundred yards to the south, "... this is a pretty distinctive place, Mitzi. I'm going to hike quickly to the southwest, inland, until I find something. There's sure to be *something*. The highway encircles the entire island. So, by hiking that way,

I'll find it."

His superior swiftness and endurance in hiking were well established, and guessing his plan, Mitzi shook it off before he could arrive at his decision.

"If you are thinking of just leaving me here and hiking off, don't even suggest it. If you leave, I might never see you again."

His astonishment caused John to stammer; he looked up at the sky, shaking—more like rattling his head marimba style—to clear away his disbelief.

"*Jesus Christ, Mitz!* I mean to come back for you with help, or to be with you until help gets here. Before sunset, help or no help. Why on earth would I abandon you? That's the most fucked up thing I've ever heard."

She glared at him—both for ugly language directed at her *and* his curt dismissal of her fears. She fought an urge to hurl the water bottle at him.

"I don't think things are as simple as you say, John. And, excuse me, but the highway does not encircle the entire island, for your information. It said that in the information packet."

He caught himself before they crossed over into quarreling; instead he knelt beside her and put his arm over her shoulder and drew her in until they were almost nose to nose. At first, she averted her face sullenly, then yielded to his steady pressure, his hand on her chin, to face him. He smiled.

"You know I can hike at twice your rate. Why in hell would I abandon my wife? If I don't run into a road—or something—at the halfway point between now and dusk, I'll return to you," he pointed down, "...stay here. I can see the two knobs from a long ways off. You're tired, Mitzi. We've been bush-beating for six goddamned hours."

Mitzi had fears she wanted to raise, but John's observation about her fatigue and the outright silliness of thinking rendered her silent. She looked up at the two prominent knobs—like whorls of petrified soft ice cream atop a cone. He was right; they stood out.

"Here. I've filled the water bottle," he rolled his eyes, the beginning of an attempt at levity, "...it'll be like our romantic week in Nepal after drinking all this untreated water."

She barely smiled—a thin response to the allusion about their humiliating diarrhea during a visit to Nepal. He kissed her, stood, shifted about his waist pack, and with "See you soon," walked off directly west, inland.

Despite his words, Mitzi's thought she'd never see him again.

iv.

For a long time she avoided the village. There seemed no sense in risking otherwise. Food was not an issue, nor was shelter. They managed both, for he could help despite his deteriorating state of mind. When they did come across the village, it was almost by accident, and during the passing years it changed. The buildings were run down, in ruins, and most of all, there were very few people.

She still harbored ill will, even fear, for the village, and they were skirting it when they saw the trio of fellow voyagers who foolishly refused to leave the confines of the village. Life was never good for them. The man was clearly out of mind, and cackled vacantly, wagging his finger at the old woman, sharing in some hazy, confused joke.

When they approached, they did so cautiously. Each time they visited, it was the same.

The youngest of the three had been laboring vainly to comb snarls from her long auburn hair when she saw both of them. She stood and pointed at them with the crude, wide-toothed comb. Her voice was unpleasant, accusatory: "This is your fault, you know. You left us."

Fearing further bitterness and misconstrual of events, they walked off from the miserable trio, heading inland. He stopped, looked back at the unfortunates after hiking halfway up a steep mountainside.

"What has happened?"

"I just don't know."

• • •

At sundown Mitzi moved fifty yards into the cover of a half dozen *ohia* trees. These stout hardwood trees—ironic tropical natives with their massive trunks and gnarled limbs—would look more at home in New England. This grove, though, formed a sturdy canopy. She made something of a hospitable clearing, hoping John would return just at dark.

After any trace of sunlight was gone, she huddled beneath the largest oak-like *ohia* and listened to the last of the strange little birds that, since mid-afternoon, had flitted about. They settled into their roosts for the night, and silence came on, save for the breakers sweeping against the rocky coast a quarter mile off.

At first, the dark was compromised by the array of stars and prominent planets above, only partially obscured from time to time by clouds, ceaseless nomads bearing water. Meteors shot across the sky. Mitzi found comfort recalling her childhood—her father's hobby of stargazing—so she occupied herself by identifying constellations. It was something of a balm to remember those times and to bring back the memories.

As a girl, she was far less interested in the heavens than she was in simply being with her father and listening to his stories and explanations. It intrigued her then and now how an uncharacteristic excitement took hold of him each time he talked about the skies. It offered him a regular bounty of respite from the boredom of being a postal clerk.

"*Understanding the language of the heavens is the key, Missy.*"

But like the night before, the clouds thickened until stars

and all else were obscured. Absolute darkness returned and the rains began—a deluge, as before. She had fashioned thick branches above her, and was somewhat sheltered. Thankfully the country was open, so the noise—the chaos of these onslaughts—was lessened.

Mitzi had wanted—and now regretted—not arguing more with John, but supposed—like always—she did not want to seem irrational.

"*Don't be shamanistic*," would have been a typical remark of his. John was a person of comfortable rationalism, and invariably used it to erode Mitzi's tendency toward the fanciful. "*Life isn't* The Iliad *or some such fable. If it only were. But, it isn't.*"

Nonetheless, she had noted peculiarities after they'd discovered the robbery, and wondered if John had also. Certainly after the night spent in the jungle—harried by the thrashings of the rainfall in the vegetation—the following morning she noticed even more untoward changes. In addition to the irrationality of three people walking off in absolute darkness, there was the rapidity with which the trail had become overgrown. Even jungle, Mitzi thought, did not grow that fast; also, though the Campbells didn't seem particularly astute, neither did they appear stupid.

"*Did you see any of these strange little birds yesterday? There's hundreds of them. And there's no mosquitoes.*"

While refilling their water bottles, she pointed them out to John, who just looked up and confronted a half dozen of the birds in a nearby bush. With long, sickle-like beaks, iridescent red feathers adorned by garish green top-notches, they certainly appeared tropical. John shrugged, but he had never been overly interested in birds. During their treks, geology was more his thing.

There were other details she might have argued, had it not been for their more immediate problem of being lost, and recently victimized. Those details were bad enough, then thngs further deteriorated the following morning by the disappearance of the Campbells. Still, during the morning, Mitzi recognized a more personal peculiarity, specifically the fear aroused about John's departure. His reaction was understandable. She wasn't known as a *Nervous Nelly*; in fact, she liked to brag about her courage; nor would she ever feign feminine helplessness.

But he had gone, and now it was dark and Mitzi was alone. She was not scared, but not optimistic.

• • •

Mitzi stayed in the proximity of the lava knobs through the next day and into the following, but John didn't return and she grew certain survival was strictly up to her,. She steeled herself to this fate through the second morning.

In retrospect Mitzi knew she could not have changed John's mind to hike for help. It was a logical avenue, and if she had brought up such foolishness as birds and such, he would have just breezed it aside and done what he wanted. But each minute prior to his trek inland, she'd wanted to say, "*John, you are going to walk off somewhere you don't understand.*"

If she had said this, though, it would have made matters even worse. Taking her bearings from the volcanic promontory, she knew that if she walked north along the coast, and the village was to the north, she would eventually encounter it. There she might take her chances. Would not simple humanity prevail? Mitzi assumed the grisly show with the sailors demonstrated an ugly lack of responsibility. She concluded the thievery and drugging of their food was a renegade action by a criminal element within the village.

Then Mitzi recalled John's recent statement about the Campbells, "*They should have stayed put. Flight responses are trouble.*"

If John didn't understand where he was hiking, why would she be different?

So, at midday, she decided to stay put.

It was a quarter mile downhill to the closest coconut palms. She became busy improving the path toward this source of food and refreshment—in fact, trusting the coconut milk far more than untreated water. Next she harvested a dozen of them, fashioned a drag-litter from branches, and transported them to the campsite.

And if a dozen were good preparation, why not more? So, she made a second trip, and had just completed dragging another half-dozen to camp when she found John sitting against the base of the largest tree. She felt great joy which died away at once when she saw he was badly injured.

"I fell. They pushed me, or I wouldn't have."

He was covered with abrasions and scratches, bad ones, but Mitzi's stomach reeled when she saw the hideous gash in his skull. Worse, at the wound site, his head was misshapen. She had no experience with such a serious head wound, and held the back of her hand tightly against her mouth before managing, "*Who* pushed you?"

He looked up angrily, his eyes wandered everywhere, and he laughed—an uncharacteristic, off-putting laugh. When he answered he did not look at her, but several feet to one side.

"Who do you *think?* The brush people, of course. Now. I've got to rest, I'm very tired. Build a fire, will you."

Then he rolled over, and fell at once asleep—or unconscious.

She sat and wondered at his state. What John had said and the way he'd said it gave her a sickening feeling that the blow on the head seriously impaired him.

Brush People? And fire? He knew she didn't know how to build a fire from nothing, and possibly he didn't either. Mitzi couldn't remember him doing so. He had been in the boy scouts and the National Guard, where once—she'd remembered—he'd taken a course in desert survival.

His sleep was troubled, and he rolled about, and muttered incoherencies. Mitzi had slept next to him for years, and he rarely if ever talked in his sleep.

Yes, it was the blow on the head all right. She decided against a mawkish attempt at fire. With his wounds, especially the head injury, she could be more benefit looking for aloe plants. But, it was close to dark, and she would have to wait until morning.

This night the sky remained absolutely immaculate—no clouds or rain. Through it, between bouts of sleep-talk from John, Mitzi would nap, wake—look up at the vastness of the sky, and looked on as the procession of planets followed each other—in line—across the sky. "*Planets means wanderers, Missy. Across the sky, along the elliptic, a caravan for us to look out upon.*"

Her father's favorite was Saturn, and hers was, too. She would take his hand and ask, "*Is that our planet?*" And he would absolutely guarantee it was now, and would remain so.

• • •

Right up to the day of his death, he asked about the events that so profoundly changed their lives. But she didn't think about that anymore, and hadn't for a long time. She could barely remember details of her years with him.

She had become so shrunken with advanced age, her appearance was more like that of a tiny, wrinkled ape than human. There was the sea, the land, the trees, and other vegetation but nobody else—no other people. And since there were no people, there was a vacancy of time. She could not decide if lack of time or absence of people was worse.

She did have companions arrive each cloudless night in the heavens.

What little she remembered of people, she knew they were not as dependable as the vast map in the night skies. They became a substitute for measurable hours because they came and went with such precision. Despite the near century of time, the lessons of childhood were unwavering. She could still recall her father sitting at the base of the telescope he'd made, smoking his pipe—sweeping away at the heavens with the stem of it, and telling her,

"*They always return. Always. You see Missy, that's what so grand about them.*"

2. There Must Be Reptiles

...Finding a proper haul-out was something he absolutely required so he could digest.

His vast reptile eye took in his narrow frail landfall and the land beyond: He'd managed to survive the crashing surf. Each turquoise wave pealed onto a jagged, open coast comprised of great black volcanic cliffs rising on each side of a tiny, delicate sliver of white sand.

It was barely a beach and more a cove.

His own slither marks—gouges deep in the white sand—marked his landing place, and his path to where he now rested. It had been another difficult time, and though crocodiles didn't ponder difficult versus hard or any such gradients, he was hungry and because of the surf, now was hampered with an injured right front leg.

He held it back somewhat, perhaps to catch more warmth from the sun. It was sunny here, warm, and he enjoyed the landfall. Across his leathery, hard back was embossed "Mama Osang's Animal Carnival" in fractured Malay. It marked him as her property, but actually Mama Osang's husband was the only person the massive, eighteen foot, seven-inch crocodilian responded to: Everyday, he fed him, usually chickens.

At one time, some true deeper instinct informed, he used to be a fine, fat salt water crocodile and he wanted to be one again. He was in poor condition after a month, on and off, at sea and with a sporadic, inadequate diet, nothing like he'd enjoyed with Mama Osang's, where people paid to watch him eat. Often, especially if a local Village Headman paid, an entire pig.

But he didn't think about specifics of food, only that he wanted more than he'd had. His last had been a panicked flock of breeding

Laysan Albatrosses hundreds of miles distant in the extreme western Hawaiian group. Now he had landed on one of the larger islands—actually, had he known things like maps and locations upon them, on the Big Island where white-sand beaches were a rarity. He'd been lucky, except for his leg.

• • •

Director Douglas Huglemeyer looked at the photographs of Captain Barleys Atoll, one after the other. A grisly mess. He put them aside and looked up at his Refuge Administrators.

"The AUSPAN treaty ceremony is less than a week off. This is a disaster."

His staff resumed their argument about the cause of the carnage while he stared out the window at the grey, treeless terrain that was winter along the Potomac.

He was a long ways from the Western Hawaiian Islands Marine Sanctuary and the rocky, tenuous islet, which hadn't been an atoll to anyone's recollection. But he was surely proximate to it in spirit, especially now.

The forlorn hunk of volcanic protrusion was barely a dozen feet above sea-level, and offered the albatrosses a scant fraction of a square kilometer breeding space. The Secretary had decided, with *his* urging, to make it the poster locale of the refuge to highlight the administration's aggressive stand on global warming. He had in fact been depending on it. The operating word was that *HE* had sold the Secretary on Captain Barleys Atoll.

He being Huglemeyer.

Returning his attentions to the quarreling about causative agents of the slaughter, Huglemeyer sliced through the nonsense—his mind working nimbly on damage control and blame avoidance. He looked at the administrator who'd given him the photo printouts; he reasoned at once that this messenger should carry the torch, especially that it now dripped red-hot pitch. Any upper-echelon manager knew carrying bad news to higher-ups was grim business, so they would expect it.

"Watkins, you head the team to find an alternative; contact the Navy and Coast Guard about shuffling around the VIPs. We've got a week. There's no time to waste on who ate what when."

• • •

Don Fujimori saw the two school busses parked at the trailhead to Alakai Cove County Park. He parked the van while the lighting director looked on with a disgusted shrug.

"So much for county permits."

They had a day's shooting ahead of them, then two more days after that, and as set-up person, it was Fujimori's job to ready the area. Another company van followed by an hour with the equipment, or most of it, and two limos after that with the models and photographer, all *heavy hitter*s from L.A, as his boss had put it.

He got out of the car and within minutes was standing between three school teachers comparing use permits—for indeed, the middle school personnel from Captain Cook had a permit for the same day and time, too.

"And ours is dated a day before yours. So?"

The teachers, especially the one in charge, looked at him and mustered no sympathy whatsoever. South Kona Productions was out of luck.

Nearby, the lighting director had gotten out of the car, and leaned, arms folded across her chest. She smoked a cigarette while absent-mindedly appraising the middle school students—most still milled around at the trailhead parking area, noisily readying to descend the cliff-trail to the cove. The teacher-in-charge frowned, "Does she have to smoke?"

Fujimori put his hapless permit away, and returned to the car; the lighting director made a show of getting back in, then reaching down and stubbing out her cigarette in the fine, volcanic soil. She then daintily and theatrically put the stub in a small case she carried for the purpose. With a final glare at the teachers she slammed the van door.

"Let's get the hell out of here. I'll call."

She took out her cell and began the series of calls that Fujimori knew could bring them to the alternative location if the photographer agreed. Mainland artistic types were often not understanding when it came to Hawaiian problems, and the abundance of lackadaisical Hawaii County employees was only part of it.

Clicking off, the director looked at the school buses as he drove off.

"Some of those little girls have nice little butts and decent boobs, no fat on them yet. You ever do much local recruiting for supernumeraries, you know, they wouldn't need any training?"

Fujimori muttered a negative response, for the question made no local sense whatsoever, and why would it? In L.A. pre-teen girls posing semi-nude for bathing suit catalogues might be doable, but not here. In Hawaii, revealing photographs of young islander girls were as approvable a notion as introducing snakes or fruit bats into the remote island chain. Perhaps even less.

• • •

The two U.S. Marine guards standing at parade rest in the lavish atrium of the U.S. Consulate General in Surabaya, Indonesia, appreciated the break in the boredom. They watched with unconcealed humor as local security people tossed the elderly Malay woman and her male escort out the front door. A struggle had broken out between them and the security people, and the subsequent uproar reverberated through the pre-colonial building. Knowing none of the national languages or dialects the marines hadn't understood anything that went on.

Peabody looked on in horror as the two Malays were tossed out—the male tumbling head first down the old Colonial staircase. The Marine guards hardly paid any attention to Peabody; they usually didn't pay much attention to anyone save the Sergeant of the detachment, especially to a lower echelon functionary like Peabody. But this was his watch; if for no other reason he was the only Foreign Service person present.

"What *is* going on?"

Both Marines shrugged while the half-dozen private security people came up to Peabody, each racing to out explain the other. They knew such a disturbance, especially with a newly credentialed Consul General just arrived, was to be avoided. The result was even more chaos, for their hybrid English/Sumatran/Indonesian volley of words was absolutely unintelligible, and the Marine Guards smiled even more.

Peabody raised his hands for silence.

"If they were so unwelcome, how did they get by all the security?"

The entire Consulate was ringed with dozens of security personnel contracted locally, forming a complex warren of crash barriers and security gates. The nationals working on these were highly rewarded—such employment meant good times, and U.S. personnel always had to protect against overzealous measures being taken. Throwing an elderly woman and man down the front stairs of the Consul General's offices and residence was surely zealousness gone wrong.

A piece of notebook paper was thrust into his hand, and two of the local security people motioned to it, then gestured back at the recently departed guests. Peabody read silently from a curious list in mangled English, with a little Dutch thrown in:

"THUSLY US DEMANDED ELEPHANT RHINOS WITH TIGGRE WORLD APE AND BIGGEST EATING ANIMAL FROM AIRCRAFT CARRIER THIRTY FEET BIG, PROBABLY SIX THOUSAND DOLLAR AMERICAN DOLLAR." (signed) *Mama Osang Bahaba Sin Lingdah, most respectfully.*

By calming everyone down, and getting the story out one person at a time, Peabody understood the woman was claiming damages against an American aircraft carrier that had somehow destroyed her animals. It seemed a strange assortment of animals, a departure from the usual sorts of farm stock.

The locals went on to explain that she and her husband were simply greedy trouble makers, and that American aircraft carriers were good for Sumatra and Sumatrans. Ferry travelers just had to look out for such things.

"You mean, she claims the aircraft carrier swamped her boat?"

The head security man gestured toward the sea with the hand holding the tiny walkie-talkie, his wand of office.

"But it was just an accident with such stupid people, of course," he said, and, bowing slightly to Peabody, he extended his hand to the list, ". . . and I shall take care of that, please to give. For there's no trouble for the part of such stupid people."

And Peabody handed it over, for even the concept of a claim over an American aircraft carrier doing local damage chilled him to the center. Clearly, the locals had taken care of things, albeit a bit roughly.

He was not well, anyway. The new-generation of anti-malarial drugs made him feel like he was on the verge of getting the flu, and he'd only been here six weeks. Another 98 weeks to go. The cryptic list, though, stuck with him for a half hour or so, until another issue came up over lost passports—issues not resolved from the day before.

His supervisor—whenever he'd report for work—would not want to confront them. A comical list of animals was one thing, but stranded Americans calling their home district Congressperson was something that was absolutely absent of humor.

• • •

Bobby "Jocko" Charles, Assistant Director of Parks for the County of Hawaii, which took in the entire Big Island, got out of his gleaming, mammoth pickup and made a quick "hang ten" Hawaii greeting to two passing *bruddahs* from his Puna Shores pig-hunting club. He was the highest ranking non-police islander official in the county government. Bobby was held in great esteem by all islanders—a conglomerate term for native Hawaiians and other ethnicities from the nearly two-century plantation industry, now decades gone.

He talked pidgin, the local dialect, with the best of them, and considered himself first, last, and always an islander. In fact, today was the day he would spend another afternoon in the schools giving anti-drug talks.

Fact was, Bobby's job was almost exclusively to act as model for other islander kids, though this week, he was the acting director! His boss and his wife, Japanese natives of Hawaii, were in Las Vegas for their annual shopping and gambling spree. 'Vegas'was a favored vacation destination for all islanders.

He entered the first-floor offices of the Parks Department onto the scene of the most extraordinary proceedings he'd experienced in sixteen years with the Parks Department. The two desk clerks were weeping—one rested her head on the counter; the other stood, arms wrapped around herself; and a third, a heretofore placid woman, seeing him, charged his way, holding a cell phone aloft and excited beyond coherence. Her voice was tight with untoward emotion.

"Oh, Jocko! Two children have been eaten by a monster at Alakai Cove and the Sheriff wants us to shut down all the parks island-wide."

He held up his hands, palms out, and ordered in his best voice-of-authority, "Whoa, there. Say again?!"

But he'd heard right, and in fact the Sheriff's office called again while Jocko was pulling things together. They were insistent, asking why he hadn't put out the notice yet.

"Jocko! We've had a major shark attack or something here, and Sheriff wants all of them down. Now."

"Attack? Wasn't somebody eaten?"

"I'll get back. Right now it's a madhouse here."

He was left abandoned of a solid reason. Jocko looked at his three clerks, again held up his hands, and repeated, "Could you tell me if people were eaten, or attacked? What happened? If I'm going to call into the radio people, I want to know what happened."

About then, the Sheriff's office, other county and especially school officials, began to route calls from distraught parents to his office. The phone became an instant tangle, and his cell phone was all that was available, until it too was tied up. Jocko struggled to find out anything—couldn't get through to the on-site cop.

Finally the Mayor came in; clearly his dress indicated he'd meant the day for fishing, for his grandchildren trailed behind him. He mimed his intentions to Jocko: he pointed upstairs to the Mayor's office, and then held up five fingers.

Meeting in five minutes.

Jocko had an unsettled feeling that he was about to be pelted with questions to which he had no answers. He felt a sudden anger toward the county cops; most of them were islanders like him. This dubious force was the Big Island's only peace officers, which included his youngest brother. Bobby thought of this sibling like he did most of the force: arrogant fellows, holding themselves above their roots.

And of the 52 weeks of the year, this had to be the week Gus Hayamira was on vacation. *Lucky Gus* was the name they'd had written on his birthday cake a month ago. Bobby "Jocko" Charles' luck, however, was apparently on temporary hold.

• • •

He swam parallel to a near shore reef and avoided the areas of pounding surf. The noise of it deafened him. Though his belly was absolutely full, the million-year-long instincts embossed on his brain insisted he find a safer landfall than the last.

For a long time any *landfall at all had been an issue for him. Hunting had too. Fortunately, he wasn't captured until he was almost ten years of age, so as a youngster he'd hunted in the wild. And though thirty years had passed, built-in instincts plus those old learned skills helped him avoid starvation.*

But he was by no means a skilled hunter. He could hunt, but hazy memories, partially hidden in his crocodile consciousness, informed him that there were better ways to get food. He experienced recollective flashes of large hunks of chicken being thrown to him— and he jumping for them.

So, a few hours before, he'd made a mess of things in the cove, entirely missing on his rush from ambush into that flock of whatever-they-were. They'd scattered, raising a terrible commotion, and, sensing his vulnerablity, he continued with great speed, fleeing into the water. Behind him he left chaos, worse than on the island with all the albatrosses, yet without the nutritional payoff.

He followed the reef line and, as abruptly as his last elusive prey appeared, he came across feeding loggerhead turtles, a fortunate change of luck. He knew the advantages of turtles from somewhere before. A half dozen of them idled along the reef, and the unfortunate creature he'd gotten was huge and slow. He made the kill quickly and the meal was the best he'd had. Or, the best he remembered.

Now, he was full and needed a landfall. Finding a proper haul-out was something he absolutely required so he could digest. He must have a lengthy, proper rest.

• • •

The Leaping Nanea Brothers—Gussy, "Fili," and Sonny, the youngest—expected people to be skeptical about the giant crocodile along Gannet Reef, but hadn't expected that officials—and everyone else—would suspect they *were* the massive reptile.

Gilbert, eldest and always the mastermind, was fortunately back in jail for violating his parole by selling phony artwork to tourists at Akaka Falls while two cousins—allegedly with his knowledge— rifled rental cars. So it had just been Gussy, Fili and Sonny who'd encountered the crocodile late Monday afternoon while spear fishing. Sergeant Kokoa and Lieutenant Mimu'a got each brother in separate interrogation rooms.

"We want to know where the crocodile suit is."

They were known as the Leaping Nanea Brothers after perpetrating the mythos of Polynesian Leaping. It was the personable Gilbert who'd convinced the wily booking agencies of both its authenticity and the Nanea family's longstanding heritage as practioneers.

"*Other leapers, like the group from Niihau, are essentially copies. We're the real thing. Leaping is central to the hula tradition with hula standards regarding poetry of movement.*"

Having the only team of Polynesian Leapers gave any company who booked them great advantage in authenticity, thereby capitalizing on the native renaissance movement throughout Oceania. It was an advantageous selling point that was now a powerful marketing tool for cruise lines and tour groups.

Furthermore Polynesian Leaping was excellent entertainment: The brothers would haul out a trampoline-like device made from pigskins and other parts of the unlucky beasts, and after setting-up, they would bounce all over.

They chanted, sang, kept time by beating on their bare chests, and the youngest two—Sonny and Fili—were excellent acrobats, mining the skills perfected during their skateboard days along the Hilo parkway. When it was all exposed as a hoax, almost a year had elapsed; in fact the brothers had provided this pseudo-authentic lore of the islands on a half dozen cruises throughout one complete high season and into the next.

This success provided the brothers and their extended family tens of thousands of dollars in booking fees, and lucrative tips from tourists, the amount of which could never be calculated. After their hoax was revealed, it was included in the humorous monologues of several national talk shows.

They were all sentenced to two years in prison for it and still faced tax evasion charges. This new development wasn't welcomed anywhere, and especially in the extended Nanea moieties. Their cousin and lawyer, Anna Nanea Collins, looked across the visitor's table at her three cousins and harangued, islander style—an accusatory hand moving from brother to brother,

"You guys could ruin our visitor industry with this crocodile nonsense! Now, if you tell the truth about *this* hoax, they'll drop further charges and you'll just have to do ninety days for parole violation. In fact, if you don't do this, you'll break Auntie Polly's heart. You three have been always such bad sons—and Gilbert too."

This all had been delivered in rapid, peppery pidgin,

of course, and in front of the two guards—both islanders themselves. They enjoyed the brothers catching hell from their Honolulu cousin, prominent in the many legal issues between the government and Hawaiian native organizations.

The last thing she needed was to be identified with this disastrous segment of the family.

It didn't take much guessing that her presence was effected only after pathetic pleas for her sons' well being by Polly Nanea, the highly regarded matriarch of the Nanea clan. For decades now, the Nanea women's curse were the deeds of Nanea menfolk.

Prison officials, or at least the islanders among them, knew the word had come down from Gilbert that his younger siblings should make the deal and get this crocodile business behind them.

A fatal flaw in the hoax had demonstrated the younger siblings need for Gilbert's expertise. The Assistant D.A., a Japanese Hawaiian who'd cut the deal, relished in the oversight with his more prominent colleague.

"If the school kids hadn't seen the writing on its back, those cousins of yours might have gotten away with it. A crocodile in Hawaii is stupid enough, but one with writing on it. Oh, those cousins of yours."

And the man enjoyed a laugh at the omission.

This was absolutely the last time Anna Nanea Collins would besmirch herself professionally with anything connected with the Leaping Nanea Brothers. After the conclusion of this crocodile business, her family debt would be paid in full now and forever.

• • •

The Assistant Refuge Manager watched his household goods being loaded into the shipping container at the Port of Hilo.

His wife and children had ostensibly returned to California to visit family prior to their move to Seward, Alaska, where he would become Assistant Marine Sanctuary manager.

"If you would have kept your mouth shut about your *forensics,* Eddy, this wouldn't have happened."

His wife was a successful naturopath on the Big Island, and the call for a similar specialty in the tiny, perennially dark town of Seward—1/10th the size of even Hilo—was either non-existent or marginal. Even if she wanted to move there, which she didn't. There was quite a difference between 19 degrees North latitude and 60. And she didn't look forward to that difference.

"I'll think about it in California. You can quit, you know. I warned you about being a bearer of ill-news. But, oh no."

His mistake had come after the volunteer biologist doing post-doctoral work in the distant Western Hawaiian Islands had run the DNA analysis. She'd determined that it was a crocodile that had conducted the carnage of Laysan Albatrosses at Captain Barleys Atoll. He'd proudly included the revelation in a memo to the Regional Director through his Refuge Manager.

Even a provisional range extension on such firm evidence was powerful career elixir to any biologist, and especially a fetching new Ph.D. candidate whom he'd personally shepherded along in her new career. The *fetching* part was his wife's inclusion in the situation. There had been suspicions.

The refuge manager, wise in the ways of government work, held up his memo and said, "Before I send this, I want to remind you of the debacle with the treaty dog-and-pony show. We're not popular. So, this bit of chemistry will be as welcomed as an outbreak of Bubonic plague, say just for example, at the summer Olympics or a Presidential Inauguration."

"But it is the *truth*. That's what did it. A big male salty."

"Oh, for Christ's sakes, Eddy. Okay, then. The truth, it is."

So, his involuntary transfer to the Refuge Office at Seward came through within a few weeks. Mysteriously the Ph.D. 'postdoc' had equivocated on her work, admitting to a few crucial sampling flaws. She, in fact, had put that in writing.

If he had to guess, his marriage was probably shot, and his life in Seward would be a bachelor's existence. He hoped getting visits from the kids would not be too complicated. Driving from the Port of Hilo back home, he became overwhelmed with resentment about the entire situation.

What good had thorough scientific investigation done for him? What good had it done for his family? He pulled himself together, however. He was a survivor and would carry on. And this time, he didn't care what strange bit of zoological trivia might come his way in Alaska. If it did, it would remain for someone else to describe. His days in the biological vanguard were concluded.

• • •

He didn't know things, in any of the accepted sense of knowing. It was far more like having them along, rather like freight. Over 800 million years of crocodile generations filled his genetic makeup with such richness of survival and behavior the element of knowing just wasn't necessary.

So he sensed that he was in an entirely wrong location for peace and contentment. For starters, salt water crocodiles, like all his close and more distant kindreds, needed and enjoyed lounging for long periods of time, and he couldn't do that here. Everywhere he went there was noise or lights, and this added up to danger—insecurity of place.

Prey was hit or miss, but that didn't make him restless. After all, that was the unchanging, primordial nature of hunting and killing your food.

Place was the issue.

On the occasion when he located a grassy, quiet estuary, it wasn't right: Much too shallow, his 2000-pound-plus bulk grounded at once, and this was dangerous. Then animals came along and barked at him. He'd experienced them before. If only such a place could be deeper, larger—more concealing. And quiet.

And of late, a mood had come over him. Occasionally, he bellowed and the sound of it was enormously pleasing to him. Then he would submerge his head a bit, and make a rattling noise that caused the water to jump and dimple around him. This was even more satisfying, and he would sometimes do it for hours.

But he needed a safe, quiet territory for this—and for everything else.

It all returned to the fact he was in the wrong place.

His belly was full of loggerhead turtles, in fact, to the point that he could eat no more. They were easily fetched creatures who grazed unseeingly along the reefs at rising tides.

Lastly, after a good session of roaring and rattling, he felt testy and would swim around looking for something to break the monotony. After all, he wasn't hungry any longer.

Built right in, as it were, he carried a simple but efficient navigation system that had made it possible for salties to travel over a thousand kilometers across open ocean. Whether they swam off to their death or not made no difference; some didn't, and now even inhabited such isolated islands as the Gilberts. These bilious, inhospitable swamps, so lethal to most, were heaven-sent for a saltwater crocodile.

But he didn't know precisely where he was going when he set off from the Big Island of Hawaii. Likewise, he didn't know precisely why he was going, save that noise and lights were just unacceptable to the peace and maintenance of his kind.

Also, where were his kind? If he had a memory—and he probably didn't—but, if he did, it was a vague, extraordinarily hazy recollection of other crocodiles.

Swimming across the sea—away from landfall—his

movements were a magnificent demonstration of form and function. He was absolutely perfect for what he was doing, and such perfection was greeted by the open ocean with the ancient approval of a blue, welcoming future.

3. Old Okata

...Night time had become special to him, without noise or confusion.

Old Okata didn't sleep at night. In fact, he didn't sleep much at all anymore. Naps. Mostly naps, and those during the day.

Old Okata didn't often speak, day or night. He'd noticed years before nobody listened on those few occasions when he did. He was ninety seven years old and had lived on the Island of Hawaii every day of it, save the first year when he came from Japan with his mother.

He struggled to raise his ancient frame from bed on this night as he did most: He sidled carefully around the young boy who slept on a tiny cot next to his own bed and prepared to go outside.

The boy would wake and look on while Old Okata slowly, stiffly put on trousers and slide into flip-flops. The boy would sit up, rub sleep from his eyes, and gaze tiredly into his lap.

He was Old Okata's grandnephew, great-grandnephew—whatever. They were most likely related through his youngest brother Bigeye Okata, who died years before, or perhaps through his sister Ikina. She too had died years before.

In fact, Bigeye and Ikina had been gone so long Old Okata couldn't remember when they were last alive, except they were living when there was yet sugar cane and the mills.

Those were gone now. And when something as old, established, and important as sugar cane went, its departure was as dire as the sun setting and never rising again. Also, you could talk all you wanted and it would never come back.

He took hold of his old walking stick and hobbled out onto the raised back porch of one of the last standing plantation houses in the old mill town. The settlement, now like him, had shrunken down to a few people who, like him, were elderly. There were no stores anymore, the Buddhist Hongwanji was empty—kept up as more a curiosity than a place of contemplation.

It had been a town, then a village, and now neither.

The last thing he did, as he did each evening, was put on the tattered, wide-brimmed hat, something he did out of long habit.

The boy would not be far behind.

Old Okata didn't sleep at night but instead remembered things.

He sat on his old bamboo chair and perused months and years as an antiquarian might works of delicate handcraft. He had worn out a half-dozen bamboo chairs during his life, and each was more comfortable than the former because he'd learned each time, getting better as he built them.

It took him five minutes of his shuffling old-man walk to reach his chair. He rested the staff against the porch rail, reached back with his tiny frail arms, took hold of each arm rest and lowered himself, feeling the old pain in the hips, back, and knees.

"*Ooooomphah!*"

He voiced this each time he sat or rose. It reminded him of times when he did speak, and was significant because it demonstrated he could still move without help. Anyway, it made him feel better.

The work bell would sound soon, as it had for over a century and Old Okata would watch the hundred-plus plantation workers come in from the field, and the mill workers join them—converging as they walked toward home.

The plantation bell sounded the beginning and end of the workday. *Pau hana* was the Hawaiian words for the conclusion of it. But it was never the end of work for Old Okata. Beginning with his father '*Longface*' Okata, nicknamed for his long, sad face, unusual in Japanese, each *pau hana* was just barely one half through the work day.

His father would wash when he reached home from the mill. The hot, noisy processing plant where tons of sugar was cooked was his father's concern. He worked in the machine shop, a self-taught tradesman who'd become as crucial a cog in the mill as any wheel for gear.

"Longface, fix this." "Longface, fix that." "Longface, we need this made." And it was always the same, for as long as Old Okata could remember. But after the end of the work day at the mill, he and his father would work in the family garden—ten times the size of most, for his father with the help of his sons and daughter operated two fresh vegetable wagons that six times weekly traversed north and south along the Hamakua Coast—the drenched, sugar-cane-packed windward coast.

"When people can't do without you, you're worth something."

And all the Okatas were worth something to those not only in their mill town, but in others. Old Okata's mother had become a gifted herbalist, growing the priceless medicinals in special soil. Her area was a tiny workshop under the house on portable tables—like most houses it was elevated in the event of flooding from the torrential winter rains. There was no place the Okata's didn't utilize to support their family enterprises.

Old Okata couldn't sleep at night when there were other issues more demanding.

Tonight the year 1934 called for meticulous consideration—reflection, to arrive at an assessment of how events unfolded surrounding his marriage. To begin with, sugar cane business had become massive, times were good, unlike in most of the world; and he needed a wife.

"You are over thirty, and you have put off a wife too long."

His mother reminded him of this morning, day, night; it had become oppressive, though he knew he had responsibilities as the eldest son. Marriage became an tyrannical word.

"*These are your family duties.*"

She would cluck away at this, his mother; finally it drove him to act. Contacting the *shimpainin* was a proper way of getting on, leaving the matchmaking to this expert. What did Old Okata know of wives? He sought his father's views: "*Father, what sort of wife is best?*"

Longface Okata thought a moment, sipped tea and replied, "*I forget. It has been so long. The shimpainin will know. We are paying enough.*"

Yet in the end it came to poor business. They brokered for a photo-bride, and she was Okinawan, and of rustic, ignorant stock. Furthermore, though his mother had picked her out from a dozen photographs, she was far uglier than the photo. Then, when it developed she could not have children, the lamentable situation was complete.

Problem was, by 1934 Old Okata was working three jobs: He was beginning to become expert with the complicated skill of efficiently developing seed cane for the plantations. Then he drove the family vegetable truck on most late afternoons and evenings, and then on Sundays, chauffeuring their brand-new Ford Bus on two round-trips to Hilo when the trains did not run often.

If Old Okata were to have conducted his marriage more intelligently in 1934, just what time of day would he have done it? Furthermore, his mother intruded into everything, and whether a wife could or could not speak Japanese meant nothing to her, for she was never a clear thinker.

For instance, it didn't make any difference to his mother if he could hold an intelligent conversation with his wife or not, if she could cook the right Japanese foods or know the appropriate Japanese ways. And how many other beneficial wifely skills were there, other than an ability to work hard? You certainly cannot tell if a woman can have children or not on the strength of a photograph.

"We will send this one back, and get another."
"You will not."

And Old Okata put an end to the issue, remaining childless and essentially in a semi-unmarried state until his wife died during the war. He never was able to be familiar with her, for her Japanese was very bad, and his Okinawan worse.

Right now during this night he'd set aside for 1934, he could not recall her name. That was definitely not right.

Old Okata saw no sense sleeping at night; after all, now that he didn't work, fatigue wasn't a problem.

Rheumatism and other ailments had seized him up, as rust might seize a moving part in a cart. Eventually he could no longer work. Ironically, not long after that, there wasn't work for anyone.

"They've come with barges, and are taking the mill somewhere. In fact, all the mills. Overseas. No more sugar on the old coast now."

His good friend Hanashiro gave him that news one afternoon and they'd discussed the how's and why's of it, but none of it made much sense. Old Okata declared, *"People still will use sugar. So I don't understand. What about the thousands of plantation workers along the coast?"*

"They will all get old and die."

And Hanashiro had himself his characteristic big laugh about that, for he tended to see life as a series of practical jokes. It was Hanashiro, in fact, who had told his more gullible fellows that his brother Yaki had gone back to Japan then returned to Hawaii in a torpedo bomber to start the war.

"You shouldn't say that. They'll take you out and shoot you."

But he just laughed more, for anyone unawares enough to believe Hanashiro's devilment just added to his pleasure in doing it. But anyone who knew the pride Hanashiro took in refining the highest quality sugar in the mill, then seeing sugar cane no more on Hawaii Island, would understand why in his final years, he was sad, even for Hanashiro. Foreigners, he avowed, would invariably produce very bad sugar. And why not? What did they know of traditions?

But Old Okata had lost grasp of the task at hand—of remembering 1934. For in 1934, this wasn't a problem and sugar cane was legion all over Hawaii, and he and others were developing rapidly the science of seeding special cane. They were heady times for Old Okata, for he was at his peak as a second baseman for the *Okimura Dragons*, his baseball club. Even his parents approved of taking off work for baseball, and everyone on his company's plantation, as did all others everywhere, cheered on their respective teams—devoted fans and supporters to the end.

And even to this day, the old photo was on the wall of the union hall of Old Okata and his teammates from 1934 winning that year's All Hawaii Championship Cup. They had swept the series from the *Baldwin Bearcats* from Maui, something that stunned all. The lushly financed *Bearcats*—from one of the largest plantation towns— had been considered unbeatable, especially by a poor team like the *Okimura Dragons*.

So in 1934 issues of sugar cane going away were hardly believable, and in that year Old Okata had both gotten married *and* been second baseman on the champion *Okimura Dragons*, which made it a remarkable year. Most would have forgotten, but not him. And by recalling it all, he felt that each detail of memory had been refreshed, as old linen might when taken out and aired.

If they thought Old Okata slept at night, they were mistaken.

Night time had become special to him, without noise or confusion. During the day, people talked gibberish—in mostly awful Japanese and then English, which he never understood well, nor wanted to. And they conversed and did things he didn't care about, so he just listened, and eventually they would go away. Nieces, nephews, grandnieces, grandnephews—and they went on: *Okata's* and *Kimura's*, the family name his sister married into. Dozens of them. Not one of them put any value into serious thought.

But at night, he could think without interruption of any sort. Just the boy, who mostly slept and left him alone, unless Old Okata insisted on going for a walk in the old feral cane fields that surrounded the house. Then there was trouble, so he didn't ask the boy anymore, or any one of a succession of them. He couldn't manage the steps down so that left him on the porch.

He would look out at the acres of now-unused fields, grown thick with knotty, volunteer cane. Despite their uncultured status, the cane still sent out its rich blossoms—pennant-shaped plumes standing a dozen or more feet in the air, catching the rain-rich onshore trade winds that came in from the northeast.

At nights, in the rising full or near-full moon, the fields of cane plumes would sway in the wind, a sea of silver-white tassels, and Old Okata found those the most rewarding moments of all. People should come out and share with him the wonder of the rich cane, with its gift of sugar contained within each stalk—each cane. But of course, no one did now.

The memory of the Portuguese woman abruptly inserted itself in this night's reminiscences. He could not place the year, but knew it was not 1934. Well, just this once he would make an exception to his rule and get away from tonight's year—1934. For despite the glory of winning the championship, his dour, fruitless marriage began that year, sullying everything.

It would help to place the year he encountered the Portuguese woman if he remembered what he was doing—and precisely where he was doing it.

Old Okata remembered distinctly that he was driving the local bus from the town to Hilo on every other Tuesday and Thursday evening. He would sleep at his brother-in-law's house in Hilo, and make the return trip beginning very early in the morning—his run carried the mail, and other important freight. Those were long days for him, but the family business was building, and in fact his brother Bigeye, always the businessman, had quit the mill to superintend all Okata businesses.

"We must have someone responsible to drive out with the mail. And I cannot on those nights, brother."

After a disagreement with their brother-in-law, Old Okata began sleeping on the bus instead of at his sister's house. The first run the Portuguese woman took on his bus was a Tuesday, getting on two towns south from his. He noticed her no more, no less, than any other passenger. She always carried a large bundle of clothes and traveled into Hilo alone.

Speaking pidgin—the plantation language between the different nationalities—she asked if he drove the bus all the time and he told her he did not, just part time. These were the times when he slept on the bus during turnaround. The next morning she would get on, and return.

He did watch her. She had big Portuguese feet and thick limbs, and looked like she worked hard. She probably labored on crews, mostly women, who hoed weeds away from the young cane—weeds that would choke it, preventing it from growing tall. Finally, the vigorous canes would overshadow everything, and survive on their own.

It was hard, dirty work.

The Portuguese woman attended—twice weekly—an elderly Aunt. It wasn't too many Tuesdays or Thursdays until one evening she knocked on the door of the bus while he was eating his cold dinner.

"I see you sleep alone on the bus."

And this is how it began, but it went on only until her Aunt died, and in fact Bigeye managed to hire his nephew for the run full time. Old Okata had never seen the Portuguese woman again, and in fact, didn't know her by name, except *'Portagee.'* And she by him, she would call him *Nippa*, after her own language. She was a very warm, forthcoming woman and Old Okata had never known that about women.

So, by an alignment of events he placed his time with the Portuguese woman: The nephew who took over the bus run was killed after driving off the road into the deepest of *pali*, the steep, jungled gorges that deeply indented the leeward coast. This tragedy took place exactly two years, almost to the day, before the war. So. That meant 1939, the year of the fatal bus accident which ended the Okata family transportation business.

Nobody, of course, knew about the Portuguese woman, and in the end, it made things only worse in his marriage, doing so by silent but glaring contrast. *What was her name, his wife?*

It made Old Okata feel uneasy about himself, for until that year, he strongly and openly disapproved of men behaving like swine, much less Japanese men who he felt were a strict culture apart from islanders, Portuguese, and even Filipinos. So, he felt that the Portuguese woman, or at least his experience with her, gave him humility, which in Buddhism was a beneficial quality.

So 1939 was an important year, for he learned to accept things the way they were, and not how they might be, and that everyone should have humility. Now he'd lost the ability to even leave the porch of his house, so this humility and acceptance were key to Old Okata's dedication to remembering and honoring each year fate had allotted for him.

The years were a priceless gift, for he knew time wasn't handed out haphazardly.

Old Okata forgot what year it was when he no longer slept at night. He instead opted to rise each night in anticipation of the mill's whistle signifying *pau hana*, the end of work.

This signal was a large bell cradled in a massive yoke, and Superintendent Mister Kelly would come out and pull on a stout line, and the striker would swing, the bell swayed in the pivots of the yoke, and the great iron bell would sound.

Old Okata had been a tiny boy, and with the other plantation-town children, he would run toward the office minutes prior to Superintendent Mister Kelly coming down the immaculately maintained pathway lined with crushed shell. He would be looking at his big silver watch—then glancing at the sky, as if double-checking the device. He feigned great drama—disapproval—as the urchins charged down on him, waving them away with his great *haole* arms and hands—so large, each was like a cloth fan.

They would jump up to try and see his watch, and he would laugh at their efforts, put the watch away and keep striding, long and slow, toward the bell's stand.

"*Pau hana Superintendent Mister Kelly. Pau hana bettah so?*"

He would give them an end of the rope, and they would help him pull to make the bell sound, yielding them some power in ending the work day. This made them all feel quite important. Then their families, in fact, everyone, would come home, yet the afternoon was still young. Many in the town would have numerous things to do that interested Old Okata and the other children.

But, years later the bell was swept away by a great tidal wave, which also took the railroad, and the bell was replaced by a whistle. This was not the same thing, but by then he was well into late middle-age, and no longer a giddy child. Almost always, the end of the mill and plantation workday meant the start of another for him and his family.

"*If we don't work hard, what will come of us, so far from the place of our ancestors?*"

He would have liked to go fishing with the others, but his father and mother would have none of it, fearing the sea, especially for their three children.

And anyhow there was work, at the very minimum in the garden.

Sitting on the edge of the porch just inside the corrugated roof overhang, Old Okata looked at the great half-moon be overtaken then shrouded by fast-moving rain clouds sailing in from the open ocean—a rimless immensity that always made him feel he was looking out at the very bounds of the universe.

The moon illuminated the clouds from above, dispersing its light in the manner of a dreamscape. Also, the bright yet delicate glow back lighted in such a way, that he could see the sweeps of rain being released from the clouds' bellies, and the water falling to earth—making all the life on this tiny, distant island possible.

"If there weren't rain, we would all die. We need it as much as fish do, but for many more purposes."

Longface did occasionally offer strange thoughts like that. Indeed, whoever might ponder a world without water, especially on islands that demanded abundant water for the lush cane-laden fields?

And as it had in memories extending back almost a century, indeed the rain came Old Okata's way. Soon it was drenching his weather-weary house with torrents while he looked and listened, intrigued. This was a favorite rush of sensations, and he looked on with fascination when each corrugation along the edge of the roof formed a single waterfall. It in turn was adjoined by another, and along the entire back of the house, the downpour formed an animated curtain of rain. This created an edifying patter on the thicket of banana and plummeria trees that he allowed to enclose his house in uncultivated tangles.

As the rain tumult passed, traveling up the wide slope of the great volcano, the runoff slowed until each tiny 'v' along the roof-edge allowed slow, lazy drips. Tonight, in the half-moon, each became luminous gems falling to earth.

Old Okata was enjoying, as he always did, the peaceful tattoo of this dripping, when he heard the bell.

It had been so long since he'd heard it, for the moment he was confused, until he remembered. How had he not recognized it at once! It's deep, serious tone was unmistakable from any other, and he smiled, as he might smile upon hearing the voice of an old friend. The clouds moved landward, allowing the moon—even at half of its full intensity—to re-emerge, spilling an ethereal glow across the village and countryside. He could see the silhouette of the mill shoreward; curls of steam rose as the plant engineer—the last home from work—vented the cookers. The vaguely sweet smell of cooling begasse traveled upwind, giving the town its characteristic scent.

Toward the town center—a post office and a dozen or so stores, including a movie theater—it began to get busy with mill workers going home and plantation wagons transporting field workers downhill to the weigh station. There they began unloading the plantation crews, the animals neighing and braying, the mules by far the loudest—anxious for the barns and feed. The bell still resonated when he saw the children returning from the office. But spotting the field crews coming downhill from the wagons, they charged toward them joyfully.

The crews, mostly women on this day, were draped with protective clothing—wide brimmed hats, arms and legs completely covered in long sleeves and ground-length canvas work-skirts. They walked wearily, greeting their children in a half-stoop, and then standing, slowly removing their wide-brimmed hat—anxious for the wash house and some time to rest prior to preparing the evening meal.

And in these women, Old Okata saw his own mother, and for the first time in a very long while, he remembered how pretty she'd been when very young. Even years after she'd lost her youth, people would remember it, reminding him, *"Your mother was a rare beauty."*

When his sister Ikina and brother Bigeye joined her, she too bent slightly, greeted each, and took them side by side, Bigeye, as usual, chattering away about the day at school, and any odd adventures he'd had. Ikina, as always, hardly ever talked, and when she did, softly and in as few words as possible.

As usual, Longface—along with those from the sugar mill—converged with the returning field crews, but he would not even greet his mother, nor Bigeye or Ikina, but continue along by himself toward the men's washhouse. He was always aloof, and even of fewer words than Ikina, for whom he always had a special admiration.

"She is prudent."

This was the highest praise his father could give, which itself was a rare occasion indeed.

Old Okata's joy at seeing all this—and hearing the bell after such a long absence—was somewhat sullied when off to one side, walking alongside other Portuguese and between two groups of Filipinos, was the Portuguese woman. She carried her bundle, and as she passed his house turned and looked up at him—not expressing scorn or joy, but perhaps something like contentment. With her, it was always difficult to know.

Finally his good friend Hanashiro came by the porch, looked up at him, and set down the equipment bag. As the manager of the baseball club, he would haul the equipment for practice sessions on the field south of the mule and horse barns.

"Thankfully, we're upwind of them, so we can't smell them, but they can us."

This was a typical Hanashiro comment, always followed by his laughter. Tonight he looked up at Old Okata, picked the equipment bag back up and went on toward the field, but first looked back, as if to say, *"Aren't you coming?"*

He wanted to call after Hanashiro, remind him how preposterous this was, but an urge caused him to stand, and he did so easily, feeling the old strength and spring in his legs and knees. His strength was at its peak with the *Okimura Dragons*. This and his agility was legendary, for he routinely jumped nearly a half-dozen feet into the air while hurling the ball in any direction—with great accuracy.

And that strength was all there again, and he descended the stairs, just in time to see from the wash-house his teammates, always racing each other in, then out, of the wash house first, anxious for practice. Nothing could hold the club back in their drive to practice.

He hesitated, and for a moment turned back toward his house. Up on the porch in his bamboo chair sat the ancient Old Okata. He would not miss him, preferring instead whatever this resuscitated persona would offer. This made good sense, for sugar was gone and his youth with it. He did not have sons or daughters to talk to—to share the old times with. And more than anything, to teach.

The wisdom and patience in not sleeping at night confirmed a lesson he'd learned long before: That no wealth or power could equal that of time and how it effortlessly moved forward and back, sweeping people with it. It moved people like the trade winds caused the uncountable plumes of cane to sway. These legions of lush blossoms turned the mountain flanks into a graceful flow, signifying to Old Okata the fragile promise of steady, unstoppable time.

Books from Pleasure Boat Studio: A Literary Press

(Note: Caravel Books is a new imprint of Pleasure Boat Studio: A Literary Press. Caravel Books is the imprint for mysteries only. Aequitas Books is another imprint which includes non-fiction with philosophical and sociological themes. Empty Bowl Press is a division of Pleasure Boat Studio.)

Unnecessary Stories ~ Mike O'Connor ~ $16

God Is a Tree, and Other Middle-Age Prayers ~ Esther Cohen ~ $10

Home & Away: The Old Town Poems ~ Kevin Miller ~ $15

Old Tale Road ~ Andrew Schelling ~ an empty bowl book ~ $15

The Shadow in the Water ~ Inger Frimansson, trans. fm. Swedish by Laura Wideburg ~ a caravel mystery ~ $18

Working the Woods, Working the Sea ~ eds. Finn Wilcox and Jerry Gorsline ~ an empty bowl book ~ $22

Listening to the Rhino ~ Dr. Janet Dallett ~ an aequitas book ~ $16

The Woman Who Wrote King Lear, and Other Stories ~ Louis Phillips ~ $16

Weinstock Among the Dying ~ Michael Blumenthal ~ $18

The War Journal of Lila Ann Smith ~ Irving Warner ~ $18

Dream of the Dragon Pool: A Daoist Quest ~ Albert A. Dalia ~ $18

Good Night, My Darling ~ Inger Frimansson, Trans by Laura Wideburg ~ $18 ~ a caravel mystery

Falling Awake: An American Woman Gets a Grip on the Whole Changing World – One Essay at a Time ~ Mary Lou Sanelli ~ $15 ~ an aequitas book

Way Out There: Lyrical Essays ~ Michael Daley ~ $16 ~ an aequitas book

The Case of Emily V. ~ Keith Oatley ~ $18 ~ a caravel mystery

Monique ~ Luisa Coehlo, Trans fm Portuguese by Maria do Carmo de Vasconcelos and Dolores DeLuise ~ $14

The Blossoms Are Ghosts at the Wedding ~ Tom Jay ~ $15 ~ an empty bowl book

Against Romance ~ Michael Blumenthal ~ poetry ~ $14

Speak to the Mountain: The Tommie Waites Story ~ Dr. Bessie Blake ~ $18 / $26 ~ an aequitas book

Artrage ~ Everett Aison ~ $15

Days We Would Rather Know ~ Michael Blumenthal ~ $14

Puget Sound: 15 Stories ~ C. C. Long ~ $14

Homicide My Own ~ Anne Argula ~ $16

Craving Water ~ Mary Lou Sanelli ~ $15

When the Tiger Weeps ~ Mike O'Connor ~ $15

Wagner, Descending: The Wrath of the Salmon Queen ~ Irving Warner ~ $16

Concentricity ~ Sheila E. Murphy ~ $13.95

Schilling, from a study in lost time ~ Terrell Guillory ~ $16.95

Rumours: A Memoir of a British POW in WWII ~ Chas Mayhead ~ $16

The Immigrant's Table ~ Mary Lou Sanelli ~ $13.95

The Enduring Vision of Norman Mailer ~ Dr. Barry H. Leeds ~ $18

Women in the Garden ~ Mary Lou Sanelli ~ $13.95

Pronoun Music ~ Richard Cohen ~ $16

If You Were With Me Everything Would Be All Right ~ Ken Harvey ~ $16

The 8th Day of the Week ~ Al Kessler ~ $16

Another Life, and Other Stories ~ Edwin Weihe ~ $16

Saying the Necessary ~ Edward Harkness ~ $14

Nature Lovers ~ Charles Potts ~ $10

In Memory of Hawks, & Other Stories from Alaska ~ Irving Warner ~ $15

The Politics of My Heart ~ William Slaughter ~ $12.95

The Rape Poems ~ Frances Driscoll ~ $12.95

When History Enters the House: Essays from Central Europe ~ Michael Blumenthal ~ $15

Setting Out: The Education of Lili ~ Tung Nien ~ Trans fm Chinese by Mike O'Connor ~ $15

Our Chapbook Series:

No. 1: The Handful of Seeds: Three and a Half Essays ~ Andrew Schelling ~ $7

No. 2: Original Sin ~ Michael Daley ~ $8

No. 3: Too Small to Hold You ~ Kate Reavey ~ $8

No. 4: The Light on Our Faces: A Therapy Dialogue ~ Lee Miriam WhitmanRaymond ~ $8

No. 5: Eye ~ William Bridges ~ $8

No. 6: Selected New Poems of Rainer Maria Rilke ~ Trans fm German by Alice Derry ~ $10

No. 7: Through High Still Air: A Season at Sourdough Mountain ~ Tim McNulty ~ $9

No. 8: Sight Progress ~ Zhang Er, Trans fm Chinese by Rachel Levitsky ~ $9

No. 9: The Perfect Hour ~ Blas Falconer ~ $9

No. 10: Fervor ~ Zaedryn Meade ~ $10

From other publishers (in limited editions):

Desire ~ Jody Aliesan ~ $14 (an Empty Bowl book)

Deams of the Hand ~ Susan Goldwitz ~ $14 (an Empty Bowl book)

Lineage ~ Mary Lou Sanelli ~ $14 (an Empty Bowl book)

The Basin: Poems from a Chinese Province ~ Mike O'Connor ~ $10 (an Empty Bowl book)

The Straits ~ Michael Daley ~ $10 (an Empty Bowl book)

In Our Hearts and Minds: The Northwest and Central America ~ Ed. Michael Daley ~ $12 (an Empty Bowl book)

The Rainshadow ~ Mike O'Connor ~ $16 (an Empty Bowl book)

Untold Stories ~ William Slaughter ~ $10 (an Empty Bowl book)

In Blue Mountain Dusk ~ Tim McNulty ~ $12.95 (a Broken Moon book)

China Basin ~ Clemens Starck ~ $13.95 (a Story Line Press book)

Journeyman's Wages ~ Clemens Starck ~ $10.95 (a Story Line Press book)

Orders: Pleasure Boat Studio

books are available by order from your bookstore, directly from PBS, or through the following:

SPD (Small Press Distribution)
Tel. 800.869.7553, Fax 5105240852
Partners/West Tel. 425.227.8486,
Fax 425.204.2448
Baker & Taylor 800.775.1100,
Fax 800.775.7480
Ingram Tel 615.793.5000, Fax 615.287.5429
Amazon.com or Barnesandnoble.com

How we got our name

…from "Pleasure Boat Studio," an essay written by Ouyang Xiu, Song Dynasty poet, essayist, and scholar, on the twelfth day of the twelfth month in the *renwu* year (January 25, 1043):

> "I have heard of men of antiquity who fled from the world to distant rivers and lakes and refused to their dying day to return. They must have found some source of pleasure there. If one is not anxious for profit, even at the risk of danger, or is not convicted of a crime and forced to embark; rather, if one has a favorable breeze and gentle seas and is able to rest comfortably on a pillow and mat, sailing several hundred miles in a single day, then is boat travel not enjoyable? Of course, I have no time for such diversions. But since 'pleasure boat' is the designation of boats used for such pastimes, I have now adopted it as the name of my studio. Is there anything wrong with that?"
>
> Translated by Ronald Egan

GREEN PRESS INITIATIVE

Pleasure Boat Studio is a proud subscriber to the Green Press Initiative. This program encourages the use of 100% post-consumer recycled paper with environmentally friendly inks for all printing projects in an effort to reduce the book industry's economic and social impact. With the cooperation of our printing company, we are pleased to offer this book as a Green Press book.